# ELVIS
## AND THE
# UNDERDOGS

## Jenny Lee

*illustrations by* Kelly Light

BALZER + BRAY
*An Imprint of* HarperCollins*Publishers*

*Balzer + Bray is an imprint of HarperCollins Publishers.*

Elvis and the Underdogs
Text copyright © 2013 by Jenny Lee
Illustrations copyright © 2013 by Kelly Light
All rights reserved. Printed in the United States of America.
No part of this book may be used or reproduced in any manner
whatsoever without written permission except in the case of brief
quotations embodied in critical articles and reviews. For information
address HarperCollins Children's Books, a division of HarperCollins
Publishers, 195 Broadway, New York, NY 10007.
www.harpercollinschildrens.com

Library of Congress Cataloging-in-Publication Data
Lee, Jenny, 1971–
    Elvis and the underdogs / Jenny Lee ; illustrations by Kelly
Light — 1st ed.
        p.    cm.
    Summary: All his life Benji, now ten, has been sickly and he
has long been targeted by the school bully, but after a seizure Benji
gets a therapy dog that is not only big enough to protect him, it can
also talk.
    ISBN 978-0-06-223555-8
    [1. Service dogs—Fiction.   2. Dogs—Fiction.   3. Human-
animal communication—Fiction.   4. Sick—Fiction.   5. Bullies—
Fiction.   6. Schools—Fiction.   7. Family life—Fiction.]   I. Light,
Kelly, 1970– ill.   II. Title.
PZ7.L512533Elv   2013                                        2012028329
[Fic]—dc23                                                              CIP
                                                                        AC

*Typography by Alicia Mikles*
14  15  16  17  18    CG/OPM    10  9  8  7  6  5  4
❖
First paperback edition, 2014

For every kid who loves to laugh,
especially Benjamin, Addison, Olivia,
Dustin, Annabel, & Georgia.

# 1

This story starts in a hospital, but don't freak out. No one died. No one almost died, and there was no blood. (Okay, there was a little blood. It was just because I got a nosebleed, but I get those all the time and that's not why I woke up in the hospital on this particular afternoon.) So why I woke up in the hospital was because there was an "episode" at school. And by "episode" I mean I passed out and hit the floor. Hard.

Obviously, since I was the one who passed out, I didn't see what happened. But if you believe the rumors, any of the following may or may not have happened in the hallway: My eyes rolled back in my head. I drooled. I spit. I foamed at the mouth. I hit the ground and released a perfect spit bubble that floated up and popped on the ceiling. I convulsed on the floor. I bit my tongue off. I flopped around like a fish. I flopped around like a seal. I waved my arms like a beetle on its back. I peed in my pants. I didn't pee in my pants, but it looked like I peed in my pants because Janice Hickenlooper was standing next to me when it happened and she was holding an apple juice box (because she's always holding one) and she freaked when she saw me hit the ground, squeezed her juice box, and squirted it all over my pants, making it look like I peed in my pants.

But again, I wasn't exactly conscious, so I don't know what the real story is. The way my life goes, I'm pretty sure a video of it will appear on YouTube any moment. The very last thing I remember is leaving the library, taking the scenic route to my classroom. I took the long way because I don't like walking by the gym. I remember seeing Billy Thompson coming in the opposite direction with his band of thugs. I stopped suddenly when I saw them.

Billy Thompson is my archnemesis. The Lord Voldemort to my Harry Potter, the Tom to my Jerry, the Lex Luthor to my Superman, the Captain Hook to my Peter Pan, the walnuts to my brownies. (I'm allergic to all nuts, but walnuts especially, and seriously, it makes no sense to add them to brownies anyway. They're perfect just the way they are.) Billy is the biggest bully in fourth grade. When I say biggest, I mean literally the biggest, because he is already five feet seven inches tall, which means he's almost a foot and a half taller than the shortest boy in our class, who is, you guessed it, me.

Billy's greatest hits are as follows: Put a frog in Ms. Parriot's purse. Set loose a few crabs in the girls' locker room. Pulled the fire alarm to get out of taking a test. Filled Pickles McGrew's locker with oyster crackers (bet you thought I was going to say pickles, didn't ya? It's the obvious choice, I know, but trust me, Billy Thompson is not the brightest flame in the chandelier). Stuck a slice of cafeteria pepperoni pizza on the ceiling of the teachers' lounge. But best of all, he stole the chalk machine we use to line the soccer field and wrote BILLY THOMPSON IS A BADBUTT across the parking lot. Only he used the other word for butt that, if I use, I'll get grounded for. Now Grady, the school janitor, is always the first one to school, so when he parked in his spot, he covered up the word that rhymes with "glass." It just read BILLY THOMPSON IS A BAD. Don't even get me started on how dumb it is that he signed his own name, but that's Billy for you. As for all the things he did to make my life miserable, I don't even want to go there, because it makes my stomach hurt just thinking about it. But if you think he's above putting a can of baked beans down the back of my pants, you'd be wrong. The "Benji, Benji Bean Butt" song became so popular, the girls made up a jump-rope routine to it.

So I break all the records for missing the most school every year because I'm sick, and Billy Thompson breaks all the records for missing the most school every year because he gets suspended a lot. To be fair, he pretty much spends his school days being a trouble-maker in general, and whoever happens to be nearby is collateral damage. But he has told me on several occasions I'm his favorite. Once I tried to explain to him that it's not very sporting of him to go after the weakest kid in the class, and I gave him that whole shooting fish in a barrel metaphor, but he didn't understand what I was talking about. So then I had to draw a diagram of what I was talking about—you know, how it's just too easy to shoot the fish because they're all bunched up at the bottom of the barrel.

He just stared at me with his mouth hanging open. Clearly he didn't get it, and then I had to spend the rest of the day worrying that I'd just sentenced a lot of innocent fish to a not-so-nice ending. Some people use words, and I guess others use baked beans. Now, don't break out the miniature harps and the world's smallest violins to feel sorry for me. It's not like I'm the one everyone picks on at school. I keep to myself and try to stay out of people's way. I'd say half the kids in my grade know who I am. If they heard my name, they wouldn't make a face like they just ate something sour. I'm first known because I'm absent a lot, second for my winning sense of humor, and third as someone who always has his homework done. I'm friendly, but I don't have any close friends. I guess I'm what you would call a loner, which makes me easy prey for kids like Billy.

Billy moved to town two weeks after the start of third grade, and we officially met when he sat behind me in Ms. Parriot's third-grade class. He took an instant liking to me. Or rather, I should say he took an instant *dis*liking to me. The problem with kids like Billy who aren't into school is they get bored easily. And when a kid like Billy gets bored, that's when the trouble begins. Billy's favorite thing to do when he was bored was move my chair when I tried to sit down. Sometimes he'd kick it forward, sometimes he'd pull it backward, and other times he jerked it to the right side. I usually ended up on the floor. Everyone in class would laugh, and my face would flush bright red.

Finally, I got so tired of Billy, I racewalked through the hall before school to make sure I got to class and sat down in my chair before he arrived. This was when Billy started drawing on the back of my neck with black Magic Marker. I mostly scrubbed it off with a toothbrush when I got home from school, but one time my mom saw it. She immediately called the school, and by the next day Billy had been moved to another seat.

But even though my prayers were answered and we weren't in the same fourth-grade classroom, the torture had not ended. Now Billy looks for me before school, before and after lunch, and during enrichment classes, like art or band, where the teachers weren't as strict about bathroom breaks. I know Billy hates me, but he obviously isn't on the top of my these-are-a-few-of-my-favorite-things list either. But then again, he isn't well liked by most of the teachers or Principal Kriesky. There are plenty of days when I pass the principal's office and see Billy being led in there by a teacher, or walking out with a scowl on his face.

Luckily, even though Billy is stronger than me, I'm smarter. I have two class schedules memorized: mine and his. And even though we had the same teacher last year, this year we don't. I even dropped band because Billy was taking it too. I had a nightmare over the summer where he locked me in a tuba case. But the real danger, of course, is not in the classroom, where there are teachers around. The real danger is in the hallways and bathrooms. It took me a week of serious recon work to figure out when it would be safe for me to use the bathroom. Billy tends to go to the bathroom a lot—before class starts, after lunch, and sometimes after school. I spent an entire night mapping out the best ways to avoid him in the hallways based on where his locker is and his favorite bathroom. All that work paid off. I mostly get through my days without a Billy Thompson sighting.

Anyway, that's why it was so weird to see Billy on that particular day, because he wasn't where he was supposed to be, which was not near me. I do remember debating whether to turn around and make a run for it. Then I noticed he wasn't scanning the hallway looking to see who he could pick on next; he had already found his victim of the day. I didn't recognize the kid because he had his back to me. But he was about my size, and instead of a carrying a backpack, he had a laptop case on wheels. Oh, that was definitely not a good choice for him, or anyone who wasn't an accountant, a computer programmer, or any businessman who travels a lot for work. I wondered if he was the new kid in school I had overheard Penny Bakerson talking about that morning. Penny Bakerson has this very grating high-pitched voice that pierces your eardrum. Even when you want to shut out what her big mouth is saying, it's hard.

I hoped that since Billy and his band of thugs already had a victim, it was safe to continue on my way. I turned my head, pretending to read the banner hanging on the wall about the school bake sale. I also put my hand in my pocket and took out my lucky titanium lug nut. It's an actual lug nut from an actual rocket that actually once went to the moon. My dad brought it home from work for me when I was five years old, and he told me that there is only one of these particular-sized lug nuts in the entire rocket ship, and it was specially made for a particular vent near the engine. It was my mom who later translated my dad's techno-nerd-speak. She said the lug nut was an example of how small things can sometimes play a big part in huge endeavors.

My response to this was "Huh?" So then my mom told me that without this titanium lug nut, the rocket ship wasn't going anywhere. She said it was a metaphor about me being born premature and tiny, and that what my dad was trying to say was that the whole family wouldn't work right without me. And my response to this was "Huh?" And my mom said it means my dad loves me and I'd understand the deeper meaning when I was older. Basically, the titanium lug nut was something cool I could show my friends. She put a leather string on it so I wouldn't lose it.

I actually won my first blue ribbon with it when I told my kindergarten class what my dad said. Yes, that's right, I won the vote that day for best show-and-tell. (It was only later I realized that during the course of the year every kid in the class eventually won a ribbon. But I did win mine first, which I still feel means something.) Anyway, so it's been my good luck charm ever since. I always carry it around with me. I pull it out of my pocket whenever I see Billy Thompson. Maybe it doesn't really help much. But for all I know, things could be even worse without it.

So when I pulled the lug nut out of my pocket on that day, I saw Billy turn the new kid's laptop case upside down over his head. All the kid's papers, books, pencils, and whatnot came showering around him, graph paper flying everywhere. I felt bad for the kid, I really, really did, but at the same time I also felt a tiny bit relieved that it wasn't me. And then I felt guilty for feeling relieved it wasn't me. That kid didn't deserve to get picked on by Billy any more than I deserved it.

Then I panicked. What if Billy spotted me and thought of me as the main course after a delicious appetizer of new kid on a cracker? I felt light-headed and whispered to myself, "Please don't see me. Please don't see me. Please don't see me. . . ." After that, I don't remember a thing, until I woke up in the hospital.

I know it sounds freaky to wake up in a hospital, and I'm sure it is for most kids, but another thing you should know about me, I'm *not* most kids. When I hear my mom's friends talk about me, they sometimes call me "sickly" or "poor dear," but what I hear most often is "special." They even say it in a voice like they're using air quotes. This is because I happen to get sick a lot. You name it and I've had it: flu, bronchitis, upper respiratory infection, pneumonia, asthma attack, bladder infection, allergies, foot stuck in pickle jar, itchy head, hamster bite that got infected, weird rashes, twitchy eyes, laryngitis, kickball in the face, spider bite, fell in bathtub, fell out of bed, fell out of car (it wasn't moving, relax), unexplained swollen big toe. I've spent three hundred plus days in the hospital over the last ten years, four months, and fifteen days of my life.

I know three hundred days sounds like a lot. It's almost an entire year of my life. Like I said before, I was born super premature, so I spent the first four months of my life at the hospital, so that's why the number is so high. I was kinda hoping they'd just go ahead and name the pediatric floor of the hospital after me (the Benji Wendell Barnsworth Wing sounds pretty good, huh?), but apparently you have to be superrich and give money to get stuff named after you. So when I grow up and get superrich, I'm gonna give money to this hospital and name it after some kid who's stuck there all the time just like me.

But truth be told, the hospital isn't so bad. Mainly because I have Dino's punch card. Dino is my favorite nurse. He made me a hospital punch card like they have at frozen yogurt places (buy ten yogurts and get the eleventh free!), so after I have ten hospital visits, I get a cool prize. For my last prize, Dino took me up to a different floor (one where he said all the patients were heavily medicated and wouldn't hear us if we got too loud), and we got to race wheelchairs down the hall.

So when I opened my eyes and saw the fluorescent overhead lights, my first thought was the punch card. Then I heard my mom shriek.

"Benji! My baby, are you awake?! Can you hear me?!"

"Hey, Mom, did Dino punch my card yet?" I asked.

Here's what you need to know about my mom. She's blond, she's got big hair, and she's loud. She tells people that she was a bear in her former life, because she likes to eat, she likes to sleep, and if you threaten any of her cubs, she'll hunt you down and mess you up. So needless to say, she's not as mellow as I am whenever I end up in the hospital. She cries, she yells, she prays, she buys a bunch of candy bars from the gift shop and stuffs them in her purse and will pull one out as needed (for herself or to try to bribe the nurses). Dino says that dealing with my mom makes him think about requesting a transfer to the morgue, "where it's nice and quiet."

She didn't answer my question, because she was too busy kissing me all over my face: "Oh (kiss) my (kiss) God (kiss), I (kiss) was (kiss) so (kiss) worried (kiss) about (kiss) you (kiss). And (kiss) if (kiss) you (kiss) ever (kiss) scare (kiss) me (kiss) like (kiss) that (kiss) again (kiss), I'll (kiss) kill (kiss) you (kiss kiss)."

Somehow I managed to push her away, but it wasn't easy. She's strong, and I'm not. There's a reason I get picked last in dodgeball. Weak arms. Given the fact that I wake up in a hospital on a semiregular basis, we've established some routines to keep it from getting boring. Lately we've been playing this game where she pretends she's a game-show host and I'm a contestant, and I guess what landed me in the hospital for a chance to win fabulous cash and prizes. If I guess right on the first try, I get twenty bucks. Second try, banana split. Third try, a comic book.

"Okay, I'm gonna have to go with allergies," I started.

Out of nowhere, I received another ten kisses all over my face.

"Mom! Stop it. What was that for?"

"What? A mom can't kiss her baby?"

"I'm not your baby. I'm a contestant. And my first guess is allergies."

"Honey, let's not play this today. But don't you worry, Daddy's picking you up a banana split with caramel and hot fudge. He's also bringing an entire jar of cherries."

An entire jar of cherries? My mom thinks those maraschino cherries are disgusting and gross. So much so that I had never even heard of one, or even seen one, until a year or so ago. Then last year my dad took my twin fourteen-year-old brothers and me out to Benihana when my mom was away. It was so crowded we had to wait for a table. I was sitting at the bar when the bartender smiled at me and handed me a cherry. I popped it into my mouth without a moment's hesitation. Now that I think about it, I clearly disobeyed one of my parents' ten commandments: Thou Shalt Not Eat Anything Offered to You by a Stranger. But come on, I was at Benihana, and nothing really bad ever happens at Benihana. That cherry was pretty much love at first bite. Maraschino cherries quickly became my favorite thing in the world, much to my mother's annoyance.

So I pretty much only get them every now and again, like when we go to Benihana (which isn't often enough), and when I'm lucky enough to score a banana split. So you didn't have to be Encyclopedia Brown to know her offering me a whole jar was not good. Not good at all.

"What happened? Am I okay?" I asked.

Suddenly I decided this was a good time to wiggle all my toes and move my arms and legs around. Phew, everything was still attached and working.

"You're fine, baby. Totally fine. You just had an 'episode,'" my mom said, making the air quotes.

"What's an episode? What does that mean? Did I faint again?" I'm always fainting. It's just something I do when I get nervous. But I could tell this was something different because when I faint, I always wake up right after I crumple to the floor, and I don't end up in the hospital.

"Why don't we wait for Dr. Helen to come in and explain everything? Now, do you want me to text Dad and have him bring you anything else from Super-DuperScooper besides a banana split, maybe one of those chocolate-dipped waffle cone bowls?"

I shook my head. I wasn't in the mood for a banana split stuffed into a chocolate-dipped waffle cone bowl, which made me even more worried. Why didn't I want a banana split? I always want a banana split. So let's review: there were now three weird things going on. First, I didn't want a banana split. Second, my mom offered me a whole jar of maraschino cherries. And third, my dad was leaving work to come to the hospital. I looked out the window, and it was still light out.

Here's something you need to know about my dad. He works a lot. So I rarely see him in the daylight hours, because he leaves before I wake up and gets home after dark. I Skype with him a lot, so I see him, see him plenty, but I don't actually see him in person all that much.

You know that expression where they say he's as smart as a rocket scientist? Well, when they say that about my dad, they mean it, because he's actually a rocket scientist. But it's not like he builds rockets, which is what I used to brag about in the sandbox when I was younger. No, he works at the place where they build the rockets, and he works specifically in a lab where they make the fuel. As far as I can tell, it's one of those jobs that sound cooler than they really are, because every time my dad talks about work over dinner, my mom makes her famous fish face, where she sucks in her cheeks and bats her eyelashes, which she says are her gills, meaning she's trying to swim away as fast as her fish face will take her from his boring work stories.

"Why is Dad coming? Am I dying?"

"Of course not! Don't you say that. How dare you say that? I'm taking away your jar of cherries for saying that."

"Mom, please tell me, why is Dad coming?"

I know that normally when a kid lands in the hospital, the dad drops everything and rushes over, but now that I'm in the triple digits when it comes to hospital visits, he just gets updates by text from my mom.

"What do you mean why? Because he's your dad and he loves you. That's why."

"Wait, where's my titanium lug nut? Have you seen

it? Where are my regular clothes?"

"Benji, your clothes are in the trunk of my car and need to be washed."

My mom thinks I should leave my lug nut at home and not carry it around with me, because she's afraid I'll lose it. But it's been over five years since I got it, and I still haven't lost it . . . yet.

Before I could ask her to go to the car and look for it, Dino walked in. Now, let me tell you about Dino. He's crazy tall, like six feet seven inches tall, like professional basketball tall. He has to special order his shoes and jeans on the internet. When my mom takes a picture of the two of us on my discharge day, she has to back all the way down to the end of the hallway just to get us both in the picture. He keeps telling her he'll buy her a panoramic digital camera when he wins the lottery so she won't have that problem anymore. My mom is a crazy scrapbooker. She wants to remember everything, good and bad, because it's the bad that makes the good so good. She pretty much has my entire life recorded in crazy detail. I know lots of moms keep the first tooth their kid ever lost, or even a little locket of hair after their first haircut. Well, my mom kept all my baby teeth (gross, I know). She took a Polaroid of each of them and put the picture under my pillow for the tooth fairy. She has the thread from the first time I got stitches, pressed on a page like it's a flower. Enough said, right? She says I'll be happy to have all this stuff when I'm older. I know she's wrong, but I always agree with her, because she's usually holding a hot-glue gun. Let me give you some life advice: you should always agree with someone when they are holding a hot-glue gun. Once my mom hot-glued one of the twins' basketballs to the floor because she kept telling him not to dribble it in the house and he kept doing it anyway.

"Hey, hey, hey, little man," said Dino, waving his hole puncher in the air. "I heard you were back!"

"One more visit and then you owe me a cool prize," I said, handing him my punch card.

Dino nodded and said, "You know it, little man." He held up his massive fist, and we did a fist bump. Then he hightailed it out of there. He's no fool. He took one look at my mother's crazy eyes, made up an excuse, and left. He already has his own big loud mom in his life to deal with, so I didn't blame him for not wanting to deal with a second one. We actually bonded over our crazy moms. One night when I couldn't sleep, I snuck out of my room, past my own sleeping mom, and found him in the patient lounge watching soccer. We competed in the "My mom is crazier than your mom" game for an hour.

Then we heard a bloodcurdling scream, which woke up half the floor. "Ahhhhhhhhhhh! Call the poooooliiiice! Someone stole my baaaaabyyyyy!" Yep. You guessed. The screamer? My mom. The baby? Me. Word around the hospital corridors was that the psychiatric patients heard her all the way on the top floor and freaked out. I didn't move at all. I just shook my head. "Great. I'm never gonna hear the end of this one." Dino took one look at my face and said, "You win this round, little man."

Okay, so now we're all caught up. You know all the major players: me, my mom, Dino, and my dad, who had just arrived at the hospital.

As loud as my mom is, my dad is quiet, except for when he laughs. But today he wasn't laughing. He looked worried, which made me worried. My mom noticed this and smacked him on the arm to make him stop. Before he could respond, the twins stormed in. Here's the best way to describe my older twin brothers. They're absolutely everything I am not. They are tall, they are good-looking, they are strong, and they are popular. They are what you would call super winners in the game of life.

Oh, here's the other thing you need to know about them: Where I'm mouthy and have an exceptionally large vocabulary for my age, they're quiet, and when they do talk, they pretty much use one-syllable words. Their names are Brett and Brick, though I secretly gave them the nicknames Grunty and Mumbles. They have not so secretly given me all sorts of different nicknames throughout the years: Baby B, B-Baby, BenjiWenji, Bundt (as in the cake), Bunt (as in the baseball term), Butt as in well, your butt, and every single variation of butt-something you can ever hope to dream of: Butt-Head, Butt-Face, Butt-Dog, Butt-Ball, Butt-Cream, Butt-Brother, Butt-Bread, Butt-Rump. You name it, they've put the word "butt" in front of it. I'm pretty sure it's just a big-brother thing, though they're careful not to let Mom catch them calling me butt-anything, because she overheard them once and they both got in trouble.

Tonight's greeting was much more subdued than normal, and I assumed it was because Mom already warned Dad, who warned them to go easy on me. So Brett just held up his right hand and said, "Hey Baby-B boy! Put it up top!"

Usually when he does this, and I try to put it up top, he sucker punches me in my side or even tickles me under my arm. But not tonight. Tonight he just let me, and he even went so far as to comment on it. "Whoa, easy there, tiger cub, I'm going to need my hand tomorrow for basketball practice." As sweet and brotherly as this exchange was, it made me nervous. What exactly had Mom told Dad to tell the twins? "Be nice, because this may be the last time you ever see him"?

But before I went too far down that road to the intersection of Doom Street and Gloom Avenue, Brick showed up and dive-bombed me in bed. "Yo, what's up, Rump Roast? How 'bout a side of noogie potatoes for dinner?" Just before he gave me one of his famous noogies, my mom pulled him off me by his ear.

"Brick! I told you not to call him that!"

"No, you said I couldn't call him Butt-Roast. Rump roast is like pot roast, right, bro?"

Brett nodded. "Yeah, Mom, I think the referee would definitely call it on Brick's side."

"Both of you stop it right now, or your two rumps will get roasted, do you understand me?" She said this in her you-better-think-long-and-hard-about-what-you-say-now-or-else-who-knows-what-could-happen voice.

The twins knew this voice well, and they fell in line immediately. Together and in stereo they said, "Sorry, Mom."

"This is a hospital—it's not feeding time at the zoo." My mom's tone was still sharp. Usually when they did their "yes, Mom, sorry, Mom" routine with their big puppy-dog eyes, Mom immediately softened.

I couldn't take the tension anymore. "Mom, it's okay. Why are you being so serious? I'm fine. Right?"

Before she could respond, Dr. Helen walked in.

"What's everyone looking so serious about?" she asked, but none of us responded. "Benji's fine."

We all smiled. Brick reached out his hand again, but my mom slapped it away.

"But . . . ," Dr. Helen continued.

We tensed up again. And then Dr. Helen told us she was going to need to run a series of brain tests to see if she could understand what exactly had happened to me at school. The first test was a big one. They were going to do an EEG of my brain.

"While it's still in my head, right?"

Everyone laughed when I asked the question, but I figured it didn't hurt to be sure.

Dr. Helen explained it was a test where they attach wires to your head and get a printout of your brain waves like in a lie detector.

"Oh, it's kinda Frankenstein-y?"

Dr. Helen laughed this time. "I've never thought about it like that, but sure, I guess it is."

The way I see it, my life is now divided into two sections. *Before* the brain tests, which is everything you just read about, and *after* the brain tests, which is what I'm going to tell you about now.

My EEG was totally normal. My PET scan (which checked out my brain cells) was totally normal, and I guess it's always third time's the charm, because it was my MRI that came back almost perfect, but not quite. Dr. Helen showed my parents and me the digital images of my brain that the MRI had captured. She said that the MRI was the most detailed of all the tests.

"Which one was the MRI again? The one where you had to shave my head, the one with all the colors, or the one where I went into the giant bread machine?"

"Bread machine." Anyway, on that scan Dr. Helen said she'd found a tiny spot, which could be a lesion or could be nothing at all.

At the mention of the word "lesion," my mom starting breathing a little heavy, but Dr. Helen nipped her worries right in the bud. "I'm telling you right now that all those terrible things you're thinking are not true. So don't go there." My mom nodded. She completely believed in Dr. Helen, and so did I. She said for now, there was no way to tell if it was that tiny little spot that caused my episode, but it might have. She said seizures were far more common than we realize, and that most children who have seizures in their youth outgrow them as they get older.

"So I'm going to have another one?"

Dr. Helen shook her head. "Benji, we don't know that for sure. But for now, since the tests were inconclusive, we have to label it as idiopathic epilepsy."

"What's idiotic epilepsy?"

"It's idiopathic epilepsy, which means epilepsy of an unknown origin."

"But I faint all the time. Why is this any different?"

"Benji, hush, let Dr. Helen talk. So are you saying Benji has epilepsy? That sounds serious. Is this why he faints a lot?"

"No, I'm not saying that at all. But what happened at school wasn't a fainting spell. Benji had a major seizure, and that's much more serious. Now, what I'm most concerned about in Benji's case is that during his seizure, he hit his head on the floor hard enough to get a mild concussion."

"Well," I joked, "if it happens again, I'll get my tenth punch in my hospital punch card. And I'll get a prize!"

"Benji, you were very lucky to be at school when it happened, so you were able to get immediate attention. But what if it happens again and you aren't at school, or at home with your mom? What if it happens when you're crossing the street, or at the mall, or swimming, or at home alone?"

"Well, if it happened somewhere else, I guess I'd fall down. But if I was swimming, I'd . . ." Then I stopped talking. I understood what she was trying to tell us. My mom got her point too, because she started doing that short, quick breathing she does when she starts getting upset, and she also pulled me into her arms and squeezed me, hard.

"So," my dad asked Dr. Helen, "what should we do?"

"Well, normally in such cases, we'd put Benji on an antiseizure medication just for a while, so we could make sure it didn't happen again. But Benji isn't a good candidate for the standard drug therapies, mainly because his asthma medication may cause an adverse reaction."

And this is the exact moment my life changed forever: Dr. Helen opened a box and pulled out a green helmet.

"What the heck is that?" I shouted. My mom shushed me and told me to listen to Dr. Helen.

"Benji, this is a padded safety helmet, which will protect your head if it happens again. It also contains a transmitter that signals for help if the need arises. I'm going to ask you to wear it for a while."

"You mean like now?"

"Yes, but I'm going to want you to keep wearing it."

"You mean for the rest of the time I'm in the hospital?"

"Yes, and then I'm going to want you to keep wearing it after that."

"You mean you want me to wear it, like, all the time?" I could barely breathe. "No way. Not a chance. Never, ever, ever gonna happen. And just in case I'm not being clear: No. Thank. You."

Even if you'd been there, you wouldn't have believed this thing. It looked like the world's ugliest bicycle helmet, only much, much worse. It covered my whole forehead and the entire back of my head too. Plus it was made of ugly green foam, and it had ugly green straps that buckled under my chin. Basically, it was a disaster. It was way worse than that new kid pulling his laptop bag through the halls on wheels. Billy Thompson would drop that kid like a hot potato and set his sights right back on me. I doubted I'd even make it through a whole day alive, and what's worse, I was sure more kids would make fun of me too. There would be no more flying under the radar with this thing.

"Mom, I am not wearing that thing. No way. Please don't make me."

For the first time in a long time, my mom was speechless. So Dr. Helen continued.

"Benji, I know it doesn't look great, but it will protect your head in case you have another episode. And that's really the most important thing here."

"I don't care if I have another episode. I'm not wearing that thing. Not today. Not ever. Mom, you can't make me wear it. I won't wear it. And you know why this is happening, don't you? It's because I lost my lug nut."

Dr. Helen looked confused. "Your what?"

"Benji, this has nothing to do with the lug nut."

"How do you know?"

"Benji, it'll turn up. I haven't had a chance to look for it since you've been in the hospital. It could be in the car somewhere." She looked at Dr. Helen and explained, "It's his lucky charm."

"I had it right before I had my episode at school, and now I don't know where it is. It probably got swept up by the janitor, and now my entire life is going down the toilet."

"Stop worrying about it—your dad will get you another one, won't you, honey?"

"Well, it's not that simple, because like I said, it was made specifically for that particular rocket and they're not—"

My mom interrupted him. "Everyone stop talking about the lug nut; I don't care about the lug nut. What I do care about is finishing our conversation with Dr. Helen, because I'm sure she's very busy saving lives, and I don't want to take up too much of her time. So, Dr. Helen, do you really think this is necessary? I mean, normally anything you say we would do, but Benji does have a point. It's pretty unattractive."

"There is one other option, but I'm not sure . . . ," Dr. Helen said.

"What is it? Just tell me!" I almost got down on my

knees. I was that desperate.

"There are specially trained therapy dogs that could—"

Before Dr. Helen could even finish her thought, my mom cut her off. "Absolutely not. Benji is allergic to dogs, and I have white carpet in the living room."

"Mom, please. Let Dr. Helen finish."

Dr. Helen told us therapy dogs are used for people with epilepsy or other brain disorders. The dogs know when an episode is about to come on, and they know exactly how to get the person to safety, and to also call for help. She said the dogs are expensive, but she was pretty sure she could make a few calls and help us find one if we were interested.

"Oh, we're interested. Definitely interested. Call right now. Mom, let Dr. Helen use your phone," I said.

"Benji, it's out of the question. You're allergic to dogs, and I doubt we could afford one."

"You'll never ever have to give me an allowance for the rest of my life. I won't go to college. You can use that money for the dog. And I'll get allergy shots. I don't mind. They have those, right, Dr. Helen?"

"You hate shots, Benji. No."

"I'll learn to love them, Mom. Please, Mom? Pretty please?"

"I'm sorry, Benji. No."

"Mom, if you don't let me do this, you'll ruin my entire life. Show a little mercy. Please."

"It's true that Benji is allergic to dogs, but there are great allergy shots that he could take, and I'm sure he could then tolerate having a dog around," Dr. Helen said.

"See, Mom, I was right. Please, please, please."

"So those are our only two options? The world's ugliest helmet or a dog? What if we just bubble-wrapped him?" my dad said.

Normally I'd laugh at this, because the idea of my mom and dad bubble-wrapping me every morning was pretty funny, but I didn't even crack a smile.

"Dad, stop joking around. This is serious. Like life-and-death serious, and by life-and-death serious, I'm talking about my life and my death."

Dr. Helen told me I should at least try the helmet on, because perhaps it wasn't as bad as it looked. I was about to say no, but I knew that being difficult was no way to get my parents to stay agreeable. The plan was to make them understand how horrible it was, and then they'd do the right thing. After Dr. Helen strapped the helmet on to my head, I could tell right away by the expression on all their faces that it was not only as bad as I thought it was, it was actually worse.

"Mom, hand me a mirror, please." She reluctantly handed over a tiny mirror, and let's just say, even though it was a teeny tiny mirror, I could still see that me wearing the helmet was pretty much the worst thing ever.

Remember how I said I tend to faint a lot? Well, it usually starts with me feeling warm, and then the room spins, and then whammo, I crumple to the floor, but I always wake up, like, a second or two later good as new. The reason I'm telling you this now is because as I stared at my horrific reflection in the mirror, I started to get warm, the room began to spin, and before I could sit down again, I fainted.

I guess my mom caught me, because when I opened my eyes two seconds later, I was in my mom's arms and I was sitting on her lap. I looked up at her and without missing a beat said, "Mom, I will not wear this helmet." I struggled to get out of her lap as I realized it's hard to make serious demands while sitting in my mom's lap like a little kid. "So either I get a therapy dog or we're going to have to roll the dice with whatever might happen if I have another episode. I mean, there's a chance I'll never have another one, right, Dr. Helen? Maybe it was just a fluke?"

Dr. Helen admitted that sometimes children do

have a seizure and it never happens again. But normally, there is a second one, and most often than not, they usually occur in clusters, which was why for the immediate future we needed to be extra cautious.

"Mom, I'm telling you right now that if you make me wear this thing when I leave the house, I will take it off as soon as I get outside. So unless you're prepared to spend every waking moment playing helmet police, it's not going to happen."

You would think if a kid faints from stress that his mom would just give in to anything he wants, and that's what would happen if I was normal, but since I faint a few times a week, my whole family is used to it. So basically what I'm saying is I can't play hardball with my mom, because, well, I rarely win, but this time I wasn't backing down. My mom took a long look at me, and then she let out a big sigh.

"I will not say no to the dog right now. But I won't say yes either. I'm saying I will think about it. But in the meantime, you have to wear the helmet. Maybe it won't be as bad as you think."

"While you're thinking about the dog, I will wear the helmet, but I won't go to school. Or leave the house. Or leave my room. Do you think I could get a mini-fridge in my room?"

"Fine, then no dog."

"That's not really negotiating, Mom."

"I know it's not, and you know why? Because I'm not negotiating. You know why? Because I'm the mom, and I don't have to."

Dr. Helen quickly sensed that this could take all day, and she had plenty of other crazy patients to deal with, so she intervened.

"Well, then it's settled. I'll look into getting you more information and pricing on the dog."

It was dark out when we left the hospital. I had been there for a week. I made my mom pull her car up, and Dino held a sheet up to block everyone from seeing me. I was pretty much near tears by the time we got to the door. Dino squatted down so we were almost face-to-face.

"Little man, I'm your friend and I'm not going to lie to you, that is one ugly helmet on your head. But here's some words that I hope will give you a little peace and make you feel better."

I sniffled and nodded, because I knew what he was going to say.

"That which does not kill you makes you stronger. Blah blah blah. You know how many times I've had to watch *Steel Magnolias* with my mom? Plenty," I said.

"Meow, little man. You are one cranky cat. Look, I wasn't going to say that. I was going to say at least when you wear that helmet, you can't get stuffed into a locker at school, because you probably wouldn't fit because your head is so big now. Heck, I don't even think they can put your head in the toilet with that thing on, so that's a positive."

I was so shocked by what he said—mainly because it was the painful truth, but also because I couldn't help myself—I started to laugh and cry at the same time. Dino gently knocked on my helmet and said, "Laughter through tears is my favorite emotion." Yes, he too was quoting the movie *Steel Magnolias*. "I've watched that movie with my mom a lot too. Now make a break for the car! Run!"

I was just about to run when I heard my mom yell out, "On the count of three, smile!" We both turned and what do you know, there was my mom taking a picture of us for her stupid scrapbook. The flash was bright and made me see spots. When I ran to the car, I tripped and scraped my knee. But I didn't care about my scraped knee. I had much bigger problems to face now.

When Principal Kriesky saw me sitting outside his office with my giant green helmet on, he stopped short and stared. Before he could get out a single word, my mom told me to wait for her while she talked to him alone in his office. I sat on the bench outside his office and pulled out a book about dogs my dad had given me the night before when he tucked me into bed.

"Does this mean I can get the dog?" I asked when he handed it to me.

"Like your mom said, we're going to look into it. I did read an article about it online, and it's pretty amazing what these service dogs can do." I took that as a really good sign.

While I sat reading, I also tried to listen to my mom in Principal Kriesky's office. I actually really like Principal Kriesky. He's tough, but I would categorize him under the heading of bark-worse-than-bite. I think he has a really difficult job. He is the head honcho of a school that goes from kindergarten all the way to eighth grade. (Though the junior high kids, grades six through eight, were in a different building.) That's a lot of kids to deal with on a daily basis, and this is his fifteenth year, so he's got that nothing-surprises-me demeanor. Plus he drives a really cool turquoise 1964 Mustang with a thick black racing stripe down the side. It's just so unexpected to see him show up in that car, because in every other way he seems like a typical boring adult.

It wasn't long before Principal Kriesky walked out of his office with my mom. This time when he looked at me, I could tell he was trying to keep his expression normal because he knew my mom was watching him.

"Good morning, Benjamin," he said.

"Hi, Principal Kriesky."

"I'm pleased you're out of the hospital and feeling better."

"Not as pleased as I am. So, Principal Kriesky, if I had a therapy service dog, would I be allowed to bring him to school?"

"Benji . . . ," my mom said, using her polite but firm voice.

"Mom, I'm just asking in case."

"Well, Benjamin, of course if you had a service dog for medical purposes, it would be allowed in the school, because state law mandates that. Can you spell mandates and use it in a sentence?"

Did I forget to mention that Principal Kriesky is a spelling-bee nut? He won the state champion-ship when he was a kid but lost in the seventh round of the national competition on the word "tonsorial." He spelled it T-O-N-S-O-R-E-A-L as opposed to T-O-N-S-O-R-I-A-L. (In case you are wondering, the word means having to do with barbering your hair.) Anyway, he's obsessed with it now, and every year he pins his hopes on some kid making it further than him. In fifteen years of being principal, he's only had one kid make it to the national competition, Leroy Fencebetter. Leroy lost in the first round on his very first word, spoliator. Rumor has it that Principal Kriesky cried when it happened.

"Mandate. M-A-N-D-A-T-E. Mandate." I figured it was best to humor him. "I must wear this helmet against my will because of the mandate by my doctor and my mom."

I could tell Principal Kriesky wanted to smile, but

he looked over at my mom, who wasn't smiling, and he took his cue from her. Principal Kriesky has known my mom for a long time, so he knows as well as anyone that her bite is actually worse than her bark.

"Very good spelling, Benjamin. Now here's a hall pass. You should run along to class."

When my mom and I stepped out of the front office, I was relieved the hallway was empty. "Okay, bye, Mom." I half waved, but there was no way she was letting me off that easily. She pulled me back and gave me a big hug.

"It's going to be better than you think."

"I think it's going to be pretty bad, Mom."

"I know. But it's still not going to be as bad as you think it is."

"Well, here goes nothing. Or maybe I should say here goes everything."

I headed down the hallway toward Ms. Blaine's classroom. I didn't turn around, because I knew my mom was watching me go, trying not to look too worried, even though she was. If I turned around, she would give me her best fake smile. I didn't think I had it in me to give her a fake smile back.

As soon as I rounded the corner of the hallway, I ducked into the boys' bathroom. I was shaking. I just didn't want to walk into class and have everyone stare at me and start laughing. What made matters worse was that my mom and I had cleaned out her car, and we couldn't find my titanium lug nut. Now I didn't even have my lucky charm to calm me down. I was really upset about it, but I kept telling her that it was no big deal.

Locking myself in the far stall, I looked at the late pass Principal Kriesky had given me. It was 8:51 a.m. And the time he'd written down was 8:50 a.m. Assembly would be over in nine minutes. I wondered if there was any way I could change the time on his note so I could delay the inevitable for just a little while longer. I looked through my book bag for a pen.

I stared at the numbers. 8:50. Hmmm, not much wiggle room there. The only thing I could do was change the zero into the number eight, which wouldn't buy that much extra time. Well, eight minutes was better than nothing, as far as I was concerned. I put my backpack on the floor, sat on the toilet, and hung out.

The bell rang, and soon the bathroom was filled with the sounds of boys doing boy bathroom stuff (I'll spare you the gory details). It was now nine o'clock, and I had to head to class. It was time to face the music. Why not start in the lion's den? If I survived the boys' bathroom, I could survive anywhere. I stood up, grabbed my backpack, and then turned and glanced back at the toilet. Dino was right. My helmet was way too big to get shoved into a toilet.

I put my hand on the lever and unlocked the door. Then I froze. I couldn't move. The twins always tell me I'm a big waffle—well, technically they call me a butt-waffle or waffle-head, but whatever. They always say I could never be the quarterback of a football team, because you have to make a decision out on the field in a half second or less, and do it with guys charging at you who want to remove your head from your shoulders. So what did it say for me that I couldn't even make a decision when I was all by myself with no screaming fans, no time clock, and no guys charging at me? I don't know how it's possible to feel brave and scared at the exact same time, but that's exactly what I felt like. Suddenly, while I was still frozen, the stall door was kicked open. It slammed right into me and knocked me down.

I didn't know for sure who'd kicked the door open, but I had a pretty good guess. I was at least 90 percent sure it was Billy Thompson. The door slammed into my hand when Billy kicked it. A shooting pain went up my arm. I fell backward and screamed.

I guess all Billy saw was my giant green helmet, because he screamed in surprise too. I just yelled, "Ahhhh!"

But Billy yelled, "Alien! Monster! Don't take me!"

This caused complete panic in the boys' bathroom. Everyone in the entire school knows who Billy Thompson is, and when Billy Thompson sounds scared and yells, people listen. All I heard was screaming and stall doors slamming. More than a few boys called out for their moms. Pickles McGrew, who was in the next stall, even ran out of the bathroom with his pants down. (His real name isn't Pickles, by the way. It's his nickname, because it's the thing he loves the most. After Billy Thompson put all those crackers in his locker, a small group of people started calling him Crackers instead of Pickles, but it didn't take.) Apparently Pickles was so scared, he ran down the hall, straight into Mr. Trenton, the fifth-grade teacher, who happened to be holding the winning entry of the fifth-grade solar system mobile competition. Grace Park had just won first prize. She's pretty much won every competition since preschool. Well, Grace Park's solar system never had a chance. I heard only two of Jupiter's moons came out unscathed. I'm just glad that Grace Park wasn't there to see it. She was absent because she was first-chair cello in a string quartet, and they were out of town playing in the regional string quartet competition, where she was no doubt winning first place in that too.

The good news is that when I fell and my head slammed up against the wall, it didn't hurt. (Giant ugly helmet one, wall zero.) The bad news is that I thought my wrist was broken, because it was already throbbing.

When Billy jumped back in surprise after seeing my helmet, I guess he fell backward too and hit his head on the wall behind him. When I came out, he was sitting on the floor outside the stall, rubbing the back of his head.

"Hey, Billy, you okay?" I asked. I may despise the guy, but I can relate to anyone who's down. I held out my good hand, to see if he wanted some help up off the floor. And for a split second, I wondered if when he accepted it, we'd immediately put all the bad blood behind us and he'd adopt me as his faithful sidekick from here on out. But instead of taking my hand, he actually spit on it, and then he kicked me in the shin. I stumbled, flew through the stall door again, and landed on the floor, narrowly missing the toilet. I was too stunned to speak. Where was this kid raised? In a barn?

"Why are you so mean?" The words just came out of my mouth, and I was pretty surprised to hear them myself.

"Why are you so weak?" Billy replied. "Oh, I know, so you can go home and cry to your mommy."

I was already down. Billy had already kicked me and spit on me, so I really didn't have much to lose. Plus I was wearing a safety helmet. So I continued.

"I'm not weak. I'm sickly, and that's not totally my fault. But being a jerk is definitely . . ."

Billy got up on his feet and stood over me. I shut my mouth. I squeezed my eyes shut and prepared for the pummeling I was probably about to receive. Note to self: trying to reason with a jerk can actually make the jerk jerkier. Luckily, someone came into the bathroom before Billy could prove my new theory.

Apparently, Grady the janitor had volunteered to check for alien monsters in the boys' bathroom to calm everyone down. He found Billy standing over me.

"What's going on in here?" Grady asked.

Billy answered before I could. "This helmet head freaked out and fell on his face. I was just about to help him up."

I just stared up at Billy. How could he lie so easily? Grady was no fool, and he knew better than to trust anything coming out of Billy's mouth, so he looked down at me for confirmation.

Suddenly I was faced with one of those moments

43

of truth you come up against as a kid. I could either tell the truth and hope for justice, or I could keep my mouth shut and hope that if I didn't poke the bear and make it even angrier, I'd get out of fourth grade at some point. Alive.

"I g-guess I-I-I fell down. Somehow . . . ," I stammered.

You know that expression you hear about how the truth hurts? Well, I figured maybe it wasn't the best day to get hurt any more than I already was.

"Well, don't just stand there, help the kid up," Grady said.

"You help him up. I'm late for class."

Billy turned and walked out of the bathroom. Grady watched him go, shaking his head and muttering something that I didn't catch, but I'm sure it was something you're not supposed to say about a kid. I held up my one good hand.

"Hey, Grady. Do you think you can help me up? I hurt my arm."

"Did Billy do this to you? That kid is no good with a capital *N* and a capital *G*." He grabbed my good hand and pulled me up on my feet.

"Kinda. It was partly an accident, because Billy freaked out when he saw my helmet. But then he kicked me afterward. So much for the saying, Don't kick a man when he's down."

"Yup, that sounds about right."

"I just don't understand why he's so mean."

Grady patted my shoulder. "There are always a few really mean kids out there. So what's up with that helmet thing you're wearing? Is it to protect you from Billy?"

That was actually a pretty funny idea. Maybe I should start a business selling antibully helmets. "No, it's a long story."

"We've all got one." Grady nodded.

By then Principal Kriesky had been alerted, and I heard someone outside in the hallway yell out, "Principal Kriesky, over here!" Two seconds later he walked into the bathroom. Taking one look at my arm, which was already swelling up around the wrist, he made a face and shook his head. I knew exactly what he was feeling: complete and utter dread. Now he had to call my mom and tell her to meet us at the emergency room.

Grady volunteered to drive me, but Principal Kriesky said he thought it would be better if he did it, mainly because Grady has a pacemaker. I think he was nervous my mom's reaction would be the end of him. I'd never been in Principal Kriesky's car before. I was pretty excited and asked to ride in the front seat.

"Benji, I'm going to try to get you back into your mother's care without further incident, so let's err on the side of safety, shall we?" he answered.

We pulled into the emergency room parking lot, and as we approached, I saw my mom's car parked right in front.

"Hey, that looks like my mom's car. I wonder if she's . . ."

I wasn't able to finish my sentence, because suddenly she was running alongside the car.

"What happened? What about our talk this morning? You assured me Benji would be fine, and less than a half hour later I get a call from the helmet people saying that the helmet has been activated? Did he have another seizure? What are you doing just sitting there? Answer me. Is my baby okay?"

I couldn't help myself. I knew she wasn't talking to me, but I had to speak up. "Mom, stop calling me a baby!"

My mom all but dragged Principal Kriesky out of his car and pulled the seat forward so I could get out. When I didn't appear right away, my mom came in after me. Suddenly the whole backseat was filled with her big blond hair.

"Benji? Benji! What is— OH MY GOD! LOOK AT

YOUR ARM! MY POOR BABY. ARE YOU OKAY? WHY AREN'T YOU MOVING? WHAT HAPPENED? SAY SOMETHING? TALK TO ME! WHAT HAPPENED? WHO DID THIS TO YOU? SAY SOMETHING!"

"Mom! How can I say anything if you don't give me a chance? Stop screaming in my face. Please. I'm fine. I just need help unbuckling my seat belt and getting out of the car. Isn't this the coolest car you've ever seen? When I grow up, this is the exact car I want."

My mom unbuckled me and pulled me out of the backseat, and pretty soon I was standing outside in the bright morning sunlight.

"Mom, it wasn't his fault. In fact, it wasn't even Billy Thompson's fault. I mean what happened to my arm. He didn't even know it was me in the bathroom. I was hiding in the bathroom, and he didn't know I was in the stall when he kicked it open. I guess maybe you should talk to him about the proper way human beings open a bathroom stall, which is with their hands and not their feet. But maybe he's a germophobe. But then later he spit on me, and then he kicked me. That part was his fault."

"Why were you hiding in the bathroom? Billy Thompson did this? I swear I'm going to go over to his house to talk to his parents so this . . ."

I should never have brought up his name in front of my mother! Normally I'd know better, but I think I was light-headed from the pain in my wrist. It was throbbing so hard I could feel it in my ears. My mom hasn't been a fan of Billy Thompson ever since he wrote on me with the Magic Marker. The day she saw it, he'd written DUMY on my neck. But he'd spelled it wrong, with only one *m*, which really made me question how he managed to make it to the third grade with such terrible spelling skills.

"Mom, my wrist really hurts. Can we just go inside, please?"

"Of course, baby."

"*Mom.*" I sighed.

I waved to Principal Kriesky and watched him get back into his cool car. Then I followed my mother inside. For just a second I wondered, even with everything that had happened, if I'd rather be at school today than back at the hospital. I thought about it and decided I didn't really want to be at school or the hospital. But being only ten years old, I didn't have any other options. What I really longed for was something new and different. Like maybe a spaceship beaming me up to hang out with friendly, non-human-eating aliens who wanted me to give a talk about what it's like to be a human. Or at the very least, I just wanted something to look forward to, like maybe pancakes for dinner.

# 4

It's funny how life works out. As much grief as Billy Thompson has given me, it turns out that on this particular occasion, Billy kicking open the bathroom stall door was one of the best things that ever happened to me. It was because of him, and my sprained wrist, that I got my therapy dog.

I remember the conversation so clearly. We were waiting in radiology so they could get X-rays of my arm, and my mom was trying to spoon-feed me some frozen yogurt from the cafeteria.

"Mom, I still have one good hand that can operate a spoon," I said.

"Now, Benji, baby. I want you to start from the beginning and tell me everything that happened. Don't be afraid of what I might think, okay?"

I nodded and opened my mouth to speak, but she stuffed some more fro-yo in my mouth and just continued talking.

"Did this happen because of the helmet? It did, didn't it? I'm so sorry. Kids can be so mean sometimes. If I could get my hands on that Billy! I just don't understand why he constantly goes after you."

"Mom, he goes after everyone, trust me. Though I do think I'm one of his favorites. He didn't even know I was in there. I swear." Sure I wasn't a fan of Billy's, but there was no sense in getting the kid in trouble for a crime he didn't even commit. And case in point, my mom, like probably every other mom in the fourth grade, overreacted as soon as she even heard his name.

"Don't defend him, Benji. You said he kicked you and spit on you. And why were you hiding anyway? What I'm trying to say is perhaps you were right. Maybe this helmet thing is never going to work out. Maybe it's just like strapping a neon sign on you and sending you to the wolves. I'm going to talk to your dad and Dr. Helen about getting you a therapy dog."

My mouth, which was open, shut very quickly. Interesting. I hadn't even told her what happened, and she'd assumed I got picked on because of the ugly helmet. That wasn't exactly true. Sure, the whole thing wouldn't have happened if I wasn't wearing the helmet, but it wasn't exactly because of the helmet in the way my mom thought it was. Probably not. Okay, definitely not. Now, here was my dilemma. I'm not big on lying. And I'm especially not big on lying to my mom, mainly because I know she knows when I am and she gets so disappointed in me, and she has to deal with so much because of me, I hate to make her any more disappointed than she already is. I'm also against lying to my dad, but not as much. I'm totally for lying to the twins, but that's only because I sometimes have no choice. It's for my own protection—basically my survival instinct kicking in.

"Mom, I think you're right. If I had a therapy dog, this definitely would not have happened." There. That was definitely not a lie.

"I knew it. Oh, this is all my fault. If I hadn't been so stubborn. If I hadn't worried about your allergies, the money, and my living room rug, we wouldn't be here right now. I'm so sorry, baby. Can you ever forgive me?"

This is normally where I correct her from calling me "baby." But I let this one go. Yikes, this wasn't the reaction I was hoping for. I assumed she'd be like "Great, we're getting a dog. What should we name him or her?"

I didn't think she'd blame herself. I mean, in the grand scheme of all my ailments, a hurt arm is barely a blip on the radar. I probably have to wear it wrapped for only a few days, which I'm sure I could use to get me out of PE for at least a month.

"Mom, it's not your fault. None of this is your fault. You're the best mom in the whole world. I'd nominate you if I could, and you'd win, and then we could put your trophy on the mantel."

"No, no, I'm not. You're the best son in the world. I'm a terrible mother. Well, that's not true, I'm an amazing mother, but sometimes even amazing mothers make mistakes. I should have gone with my gut. I knew the helmet was not going to end well, and I should have just listened to my inner voice."

"So can we get a dog?"

"Well, I've got to talk to your father first."

This is actually something my mom likes to say a lot, but in the whole history of my life on this planet, I have never once experienced my dad saying no to my mom about anything she wants. It's not that Dad's a big pushover. Well, he is, but he's not a wimp about it. He just thinks my mom is supersmart and capable, and he knows that if she thinks it's the right thing to do, then it probably is.

My mom went to find Dr. Helen, while I waited for my name to be called. She told me to think about what kind of banana split I wanted, because right after the hospital we were heading over to SuperDuperScooper.

"Can I have five cherries?"

"Don't push your luck. You can have two."

"Three?"

"Two."

"Okay, two it is. That's all I really wanted anyway, Mom." I was fine with two. I could have pushed her to get three, but now that I was getting my dog, the number of cherries didn't matter so much.

About five minutes passed, and I was busy finding hidden objects in a picture in an old *Highlights* magazine. I found everything almost immediately, and I couldn't believe there was a time when I'd struggled to find everything. I heard him before I saw him. It was Dino's booming voice, but this wasn't the regular, happy Dino—this was something else entirely. I had never heard him talk like this before.

"I'm telling you this is a waste of time," he said.

"She's *my* daughter, and I know what's good for her."

"Yeah, well, she's my favorite niece, and I think I know a little more than you when it comes to this sort of thing."

"You're not even a doctor. You're just a nurse."

I hadn't looked up from my magazine, mainly because I was a chicken and there's nothing I hate more than people yelling, but curiosity finally won out. What I saw was surprising, because I'm always used to Dino being the biggest guy in every room. The man arguing with Dino was even taller and wider than Dino. They looked like they were related. I remembered Dino telling me that he had a much older half brother. Maybe this was him.

"Yes, I am a nurse, a great nurse. You got a problem with that?"

"Daddy, Uncle Dino, stop it right now!"

Again, I heard and recognized the voice before I saw her. I saw two hands pushing apart the two men, and standing between them was Taisy McDonald. Taisy McDonald, the tallest girl in the fourth grade. Taisy McDonald, who was the only daughter of Big Tate McDonald, a two-time Super Bowl champion and local celebrity in these parts. Taisy is the best female athlete in our entire town. When she was only six years old, she was one of the top gymnasts in the under-ten category in the entire country. Then I guess she hit a crazy growth spurt when she turned nine, and she grew too big to be an Olympic hopeful. But even though her gymnastics career was over, every-one knew all she had to do was pick out what other sport was lucky enough to get her. She's kind of like the twins, meaning she plays every single sport well. Instead of playing just girls' soccer or softball, she's so good all the boys' sports teams in town want her as well. She's also a year older than the rest of us in fourth grade, but that's because she missed so much school with all her training.

I couldn't believe I hadn't known that Dino was Taisy McDonald's uncle. I also couldn't believe that Dino looked small compared to her father. Well, maybe not small, but he was now the second biggest guy in the room. Whenever I'm in the hospital, I never really talk about school much with Dino, and it's not like Taisy and I are friends, though we've had a few enrichment classes together.

"You two, take it out into the hallway! You're embarrassing me." And with that, Taisy actually pushed both of them toward the door. It was a pretty funny sight to see a young girl bossing around two huge men.

"Taisy, stop it. Why don't you sit here while your uncle and I go to the cafeteria? Do you want something?"

"May I please have a soda?"

"No, you may not have a soda. I'll get you some fruit and water."

"Then why did you even ask me what I wanted? What about some Vitaminwater? I like every color but orange."

"Anything else? A bendy straw, perhaps?" her dad said sarcastically.

"Stop being snarky, Daddy, or I'll tell Mom on you. And yes, I'd love a bendy straw if possible. And you be nice to Uncle Dino."

Dino and Taisy's father left. By then, pretty much all eyes were on her, and she knew it. She looked at the floor and walked over to the corner of the room, taking a seat right across from me. I quickly looked down at the picture open in front of me and found the last object I had been looking for, an owl. Then I heard her crying softly. Looking up, I saw her head hanging low. She was sniffling.

My mom has always put a little Kleenex packet in the front zippered pocket of my backpack. I never ever use it, and I always tell her I don't need it, but she always puts it in there. "Benji, honey," she says, "you never know when you might run into a damsel in distress who needs a hankie." And I always say back, "Yeah, Mom, because my life is exactly like a fairy tale." Well, score one for my mom, because I guess this was the moment she was talking about.

I took out the tissue packet and walked over and held it out for Taisy. She looked up at me and said in the saddest voice I've ever heard, "Thanks." And then she said, "I've never seen a tissue with a duck on it before."

I looked at the packet, and sure enough, there was a yellow duck with a red bow tie printed right on every tissue. Oh great, why can't my mom ever be normal? Who buys tissues with ducks on them?

"Oh, I, uh, well, my mom got them. I guess. They're kinda lame, I guess."

"They're not lame. I like them. They're supercute. Though I feel bad that I just blew my nose all over the duck."

I guess I was really nervous, but there was something about this that cracked me up, and I knew it wasn't the right time or place to laugh, but that only made me laugh harder. I felt bad about laughing, but I'm happy to report that Taisy joined in, which was cool, because she always seems so serious. She motioned for me to sit down next to her, and I did.

She noticed my sling that one of the emergency room attendants had given me. "What happened to your arm?"

"I kinda got into a thing with Billy Thompson in the bathroom."

"You fought Billy Thompson?"

For a moment I considered saying yes, because maybe Taisy would think I was tougher than I looked if she thought I got into fights in bathrooms, but she was probably too smart to believe it.

"Not exactly. It was an accident, kind of."

"I don't think there are any accidents when it comes to Billy Thompson." Taisy said it with such certainty; I knew there was a story behind her words.

"Does he pick on you too?"

"Not really. He knows better. But he glued my friend Annabel's locker shut once for no reason at all. And my friend Georgia swears he stole her favorite gold glitter pen. I was with her when she confronted him, and he had gold glitter all over his fingers, but he still denied it! For some reason he doesn't have to take gym, and I hear that's when he goes around the school stealing things from lockers."

"Jerk, thief, liar. Yep, that sounds about right." I knew I sounded a little bitter, but I couldn't help it. I'm one of the few kids who actually like school, so it always burns me up that he manages to ruin at least one day a week for me. "Can we change the subject now? Just talking about him puts a bad taste in my mouth."

She nodded. "Should I ask about the helmet?"

Oh no, with all the craziness that happened, I had forgotten I was still wearing it. "Please don't."

She nodded, and I could tell she understood. I wondered if I should ask her about what had just happened. Instead, I went the safer route.

"What are you in for?" I know that sounds overly dramatic, like we were both in prison, but she doesn't know me at all, so it felt liberating that I could pretend to be cooler than I was.

"My dad wants me to get my elbow x-rayed, because my free throw's a bit off lately."

I waited to see if she'd say anything more, but I didn't want to push, because she didn't push me about my helmet head.

"Can you keep a secret?" Taisy whispered.

"Of course."

"Pinkie swear secret?"

I held out my good hand and raised my pinkie. "Pinkie swear." My heart was racing at the thrill of a secret. I took a deep breath so I wouldn't get overly excited and faint.

"I've been messing up on purpose, and when my

dad asked me what was going on, I lied and said my elbow felt funny. He freaked out and dragged me down here. Now it's a big mess, because there's actually nothing wrong with my elbow at all."

"Why would you lie?"

"Did you know I play sports?"

"Taisy, everyone in the world knows you play sports. You were on the cover of *Sports Illustrated* when you were eight."

"That's true, but it's not like I was the only kid on the cover. There was a kid from every state—I was just the kid from Pennsylvania. We were all supposed to be these 'elite'"—she used air quotes—"child athletes." But six months later I got too big for gymnastics, and it was over for me. Just like that." She snapped her fingers. "And ever since, my dad keeps pushing me to try all these other sports like tennis, golf, basketball, and one morning I woke up to find he put a volleyball court in our backyard, but that's cool now because we use it for badminton, which I love. It's like he's determined to make me a champion again and . . ."

"And what?"

"And I'm just kind of sick of it. I really loved gymnastics, so it was disappointing when I got too tall. But it's not like I'm a light switch and he can turn me on and off when it comes to any other sports, you know? And I used to get invited to birthday parties, but they were always on the weekends when I was playing in tournaments, so I never got to go. Now I don't even get invited anymore. I don't want to wear sneakers all the time and ponytails. I want to wear dresses to school and do my hair cute like other girls. I'm tired of being sweaty and having to high-five everyone. I dunno, I guess I just want to be normal and have fun and hang out. This must sound so stupid to you."

"Nope. I definitely get wanting to be normal."

"What should I do? Do I get the X-ray? Do I tell my dad I lied? I hate it when he's disappointed in me. I'm so mad at myself for making everything such a big mess. The lie just came out, and I thought he'd let me relax a little, but instead it had the opposite effect." She started to cry again. I handed her the ducky tissues again.

"I can't say I know what you're going through. But I can say this. Your uncle is my favorite nurse here at the hospital, and as you may or may not know, I spend a lot of time here. I'd talk to him if you don't want to talk to your dad. Maybe he can help." I paused, and then said, "Or maybe that might make things worse, because your dad would just get mad at Dino and they might get into a fight, and if Dino gets a busted lip, I'd feel terrible. But if he did get a busted lip, he'd at least know what to do with it, since he's a nurse. Okay, I guess I'm not all that helpful. Most people don't tend to ask for my advice."

Taisy smiled.

"You're pretty funny, Benj." She stood up. "I'm going to go find them and talk to them. It's my life. If I want to take some time off from sports, I should be able to say so. Just because my dad and my mom were champion athletes doesn't mean I have to be, right?"

I admired her quick decision and her bravery. The twins would never accuse her of being a waffle-butt. She suddenly seemed exactly like the confident and supercool Taisy who proudly walked around the school hallways. She held out the ducky tissues packet for me to take. I shook my head and gently pushed them back to her.

"You keep them. To remember me by."

It sounded better in my head than when I said it out loud. But that's because I think it's some piece of corny movie dialogue from some corny movie that my mom watches. I couldn't believe I'd just said that. Why would I say that? I was immediately embarrassed, but before I could regret it too much, Taisy laughed again.

"You're too funny."

And just like that, she was gone. I was still staring at the doorway after her when my mom showed up again.

"Awwwww, is that goofy smile for me? Did you miss me? I tried to hurry."

I didn't have the heart to tell her that my smile was for some other girl, so I nodded.

So I'm skipping over the majority of the two long and boring weeks it took for me to get my dog, mainly because they were the longest, most boring days in the history of the world. Dr. Helen had written me a note so I missed school while I was waiting. All my teachers sent me my homework over email. Every morning I did my homework, and by lunchtime I was free to stare at the clock on the kitchen microwave, hoping that time would pass more quickly.

Even though the days were long and boring, the nights were a little different. Like I said before, the twins were the exact opposite of me, so where I saw my helmet as one of the worst things to ever happen to me, the twins saw it as one of the best things that ever happened to them. You think your older siblings torture you sometimes? Well, trust me, that's nothing compared to my brothers.

The morning after I got the helmet, I woke up to find that they had taken off the tusks of Stinky Tuskadero (my mom named him for me), my gray stuffed elephant, and glued them to either side of my helmet so I looked like a Viking. Brett called me Sir Buttsky Buttsby and saluted me. I told them Vikings didn't have titles like "Sir," nor were they saluted. Brick thought it was hilarious that I corrected Brett and started laughing at him. Pretty soon they were rolling around on my floor like wild animals.

On the second night, they painted the helmet silver and attached the antennae from an old TV we have in the basement on top of it. That was Brick's brilliant idea, but he wasn't in my room when I woke up the next morning, because he got silver paint all over mom's glue gun and stayed up really late trying to scrape it off before she busted him. What he should have realized was they were always going to get busted. I found it pretty funny he even bothered to try to clean off the evidence.

On the third night, despite the fact that my mom had threatened them both, they decided to risk getting grounded anyway. They taped a bunch of magnets to the helmet, convinced that whenever I passed something made of metal, it would stick to my head. What they didn't realize was that while trying to tape on the magnets, the digital alarm in my helmet got triggered.

The medical alarm company was alerted. They immediately called my mom in the middle of the night. I woke up during all the commotion, got totally disoriented by everyone in my room yelling about the alarm company, and assumed something really bad had happened. Then I fainted, fell off my bed, landed funny, and had to go to the emergency room to see if I'd broken my other wrist. I hadn't broken it, but while I was there, they checked out my first sprained wrist, and it was much better, so the nurse just switched my sling from one arm to the other one.

Needless to say, the twins got into big trouble. First, my mom put them on dishwashing duty for a month. But on the first day they broke my dad's favorite coffee mug, so that was over pretty quick. Then she grounded them for two weekends in a row but quickly realized if they weren't playing football on the weekends with their friends and getting all tired out, the coffee cup wouldn't be the only thing broken. The twins were not the type of kids who would do well caged up. Finally, my mom got creative. She dyed and painted all their sports equipment purple. That's right—the basketballs, the footballs, their lacrosse sticks, even the tennis balls. She also dyed their underwear and athletic cups. She said they'd see exactly what it felt like to get teased when they were in the locker room. What my mom didn't know was that they are both so popular that it's highly unlikely that even purple underwear would get them teased at school. They'd probably just start a new fashion trend with their purple football pants.

Being a little brother, I'm used to the twins torturing me. Honestly, it doesn't even bother me all that much. I know they're just kidding around. When Billy comes after me at school, I know his goal is to make me miserable, but the twins are really just trying to be funny. My brothers aren't big on words, and this is their way of showing me they care. At least, that's what my dad told me when my mom sent him in to talk to me.

The night before my new dog arrived, I was so excited I couldn't sleep. He was trained in Tennessee at a special farm. Service dogs have lots of skills, and they help a lot of different people. There are service dogs for people who are blind or deaf, for people who have seizures, for people unable to walk. Dr. Helen told us that some dogs are trained to know when a person is about to have a heart attack. When I asked how you train a dog to learn that, Dr. Helen told me she had no idea, but that dogs are the most attuned to human emotions out of all the other animals in the world. I guess there are animals that are smarter than dogs, like orangutans and chimps, but when it comes to empathy, dogs are the best.

Dr. Helen described the farm like a college for dogs. A lot of dogs go, but only a few ever graduate. Some dogs train for more than two years. The father of one of her former patients used to train dogs for the army, but now he's one of the head trainers at the farm. His name is Action Jaxin, and she said he's famous in the dog training world. His daughter Lola Beth was born premature like me and weighed even less than I did. I guess it's a good thing Dr. Helen has saved so many of her patients' lives, because they are all very grateful and would do anything for her, like let me skip the waiting list and get my dog right away.

As long and boring as those fourteen days were, the day the dog arrived was even longer. I camped out at the bay window in our living room from eight in the morning on. It's the best view of the street in front of our house, and it's really cozy, because Mom made a supersoft and thick pillow cushion for it, and she even put in a cup holder. I'm serious, she really did put one in, right into the cushion. Mom says that having a house full of boys means you have to be a little more creative if you want to have nice things.

Anyway, I waited, and waited, and waited until eventually I got all warm and toasty sitting in the sun and fell asleep with my face pressed up against the glass. The only good thing I can say about this giant ugly helmet is that it was like having a pillow built into your head. And when I say only, I definitely mean only.

I woke up to the sound of the doorbell. Bolting off the cushion, I ran to the door. It took me a minute to realize why the delivery guys were looking at me funny. Duh, I had the helmet on. I also had an indentation from the window across my cheek. I unbuckled my helmet and threw it to the side.

"Mom! Mom! My dog's here!! He's finally, finally here!!"

One of the delivery guys wheeled in a crate so massive I couldn't see my new dog yet. My mom came downstairs to sign the paperwork, took one look at the size of the crate, and immediately started freaking out.

"Wait a second. What's in there? A dog, or a pony?

Why is the crate so big? How do we even know there's a dog in there? Do you transport other animals? The last thing I need is to open that crate and have a tiger come out and maul my son."

The delivery guys were obviously tired from their long drive, and they ignored my mom. They told her it was definitely a dog, because they walked it an hour ago. And size was not their department. Their job was done as soon as she signed the paper.

I sprang into action at this point, by grabbing the pen and clipboard from the guy and thrusting it into my mom's hands.

"Mom, sign the paper. C'mon! Sign the paper. These guys are tired. They've been driving for days. They want to go home and see their wives and kids."

My mom laughed and signed the paper. The guys took their clipboard and left. Okay, I will now admit that I was a little surprised at the size of the crate too. It was huge. Like almost four feet tall.

I unlocked the crate, and the door swung open. Two dark eyes stared out at me. I slowly backed away from the crate, and as I did, the biggest, blackest dog I've ever seen walked out of the crate. He was huge. His head was huge, way bigger than my head. All I could manage to say was "Whoa." But I didn't have to say anything, because my mom started saying everything for me.

"What the— Oh my goodness— Look at the size of his— I've never seen such a big— There has to be a mistake because that dog is— I knew I shouldn't have signed that paper before I— I should go call someone. There must be a mistake. Benji, whatever you do, do not let that horse-size dog pee on my white carpet." And then she ran to the kitchen to go make a phone call.

Meanwhile, the dog walked around our living room, smelling the furniture, smelling the carpet, circling the couch. Finally he came right up to me and opened his mouth. Then the biggest tongue I've ever seen up close and personal (as opposed to on the Discovery Channel or Animal Planet Channel) came out of his mouth and licked my face. The tongue was so big, it almost knocked me over.

I put my good hand in front of his nose, which is what I read online that you're supposed to do when you first meet a new dog. It's so the dog can get used to my smell and know that I'm friendly. Only then can you move to pet his head. His fur was silky smooth and thick.

"Hi, doggy. My name is Benji. What's your name, huh?"

The dog opened his mouth again. I thought he was

going to lick the other half of my face, but instead he said, "Very nice to meet you, Benji. My name is Parker Elvis Pembroke IV. You may call me Parker Elvis Pembroke. Or Mr. Pembroke, if you prefer. So . . . this place is much smaller than I imagined."

Okay, I know what you're thinking. You're thinking, did I just read that correctly? Did he say the dog talked? Well, I'm here to tell you that you did read correctly, and yes, the dog did talk, and that's exactly what he said, word for word. But if you're surprised, you should be, because when it happened, I was just as surprised as you are. So much so that I didn't even know what to say. My first thought was that the twins were playing a joke on me, and my second thought was that perhaps I was having some weird allergic reaction to the dog, and my third thought was that I'd imagined the whole thing, because I'm a pretty smart kid and I know that *dogs do not talk!*

I would have totally gone with number three, but then the dog, or rather Parker Elvis Pembroke IV, cleared his throat.

"Excuse me, did you hear what I said? I said this place is much smaller than I imagined. Do"—pause—"you"—pause—"know"—pause—"how"—pause—"to"—pause—"talk, young man?"

I found this really weird, because the dog was talking like *I* was the weird one.

"Yes, I can talk. I'm a human, and we're supposed to talk. But are you talking? Because you're a dog, and I didn't think you could talk. I'm kind of surprised by all of this. You are talking, right? Or am I having an episode? And if I'm having an episode, I don't know how good a job you're doing helping me. I feel like it's warm in here, are you warm? You have lots of hair, so maybe you're warm all the time, but I think . . ."

And then I fainted. I woke up a second later, lying on the couch with the dog licking my face. I took a deep breath. Okay, maybe I got a little overexcited that the dog had finally arrived, and I just fainted like how I always faint, and then I had a dream that the dog talked, and then I woke up.

This is when the dog opened his mouth and said, "Are you okay, young man? It appears you fainted."

So much for this being a crazy dream.

"I'm okay. I faint all the time. It's kind of no big deal around here."

"But why did you faint? Was it something I said? Are you ill? May I fetch you anything?"

"Yes, in fact it was something you said. I mean, not what you said, but that you said anything at all. Dogs don't normally talk. I guess you're the first dog I've ever had, so I'm no expert, but I'm pretty sure I would have heard if dogs could talk."

"Well, I can't speak for all dogs. But I can talk. Well, let me rephrase that. All dogs can talk to one another. And I can certainly talk to anyone, but most people don't understand me when I do, so I guess that makes you special."

There was that word again, "special." What I wouldn't give to just be regular.

"So did someone tell you my house would be bigger than it is?"

"No one told me *your* house would be bigger than this, because I don't even know you. We just met. What I am merely trying to explain is that I read many books about this place so as to be prepared for my stay, and it looks very different from what I imagined in my head. So are we in the East Wing? Or the West Wing? Perhaps we are in the house staff quarters? Did I need to come through the delivery entrance for security purposes? I suppose that would be normal protocol upon entry here. I know: Are you a child of one of the employees?"

Now I was totally lost. I mean, it's confusing enough to have a dog talking to you, but then to have him talk to you and have no clue what exactly he's talking about is off-the-charts confusing.

"East wing? We don't really have an east wing. Or a west wing, for that matter. We do have an upstairs and a partially finished basement. But there is one creaky step on the way down, and I keep asking my dad whether it's about to give way. He keeps saying that it's just creaky, but I have my suspicions. And you're so big, I'd hate it if my dad was wrong and you crashed right through the step."

Now he was confused too, because he tilted his head to one side and gave me that funny dog confused look. After another second, he tilted it to the other side. I couldn't help but wonder whether he was thinking which arm of mine would taste better as an appetizer. As soon as he started speaking, I could tell he was a little cranky. He really spoke his words very clearly for a dog. In fact, he sounded like those boring Shakespeare movies that my dad watches on the BBC or a butler on a TV show.

"Is this, or is this not, sixteen hundred Pennsylvania Avenue?"

Sixteen hundred Pennsylvania Avenue? Sixteen hundred Pennsylvania Avenue? Why was that address so familiar? Then it clicked.

"Isn't that the address of the White House?"

"Precisely."

"You mean like the White House where the president of the United States lives?" I laughed.

"That's exactly what I mean. Why are you laughing? I don't find this situation amusing enough to warrant laughter at all. Perhaps I could speak with your superior officer? Your supervisor? Or perhaps your trainer?"

"I don't have a trainer. Do you mean my mom? I can get her if you want me to, but I think she's calling the place where we got you, because you're bigger than you're supposed to be. We were expecting a regular-sized dog as opposed to a supersized one. You're the biggest dog I've ever seen in my entire life. Not that I've seen that many dogs up close, mind you. I have allergies." And as if on cue, I sneezed. "Hey, how much do you weigh?"

"My weight is none of your business. How would you feel if I asked you how much you weigh?"

"I have no problem with you asking me. I'd tell you I weigh about fifty pounds, give or take a few pounds."

"I weigh more than that. Maybe even three to four times as much, but I have big bones, and my breed is what you would call a large breed. I'm a Newfoundland, and male Newfoundland dogs run anywhere between one hundred fifty and two hundred pounds. I am not fat, I am regal. Well, technically, regal means of royal lineage, and I'm not claiming that per se, but I was using the term in a more casual way."

"Whoa, whoa, whoa, no one here is calling anyone fat. I don't think you're fat at all."

As I said all this, I thought, Just my luck, I have a talking dog who isn't very friendly, who has a head that weighs the same as my entire body, and who also happens to be sensitive about his weight.

"You are correct, and I apologize. I've had a terribly long and trying two days. I was stuck in a dark crate in the back of an SUV, and the drivers, don't even get me started on their terrible taste in music. I kept hoping they would turn the station to NPR, but instead they listened to heavy metal and sports radio. Anyway, moving on, am I in Washington, DC, at the White House or not?"

"Not. You are in Wyncote, Pennsylvania. Forty-one thirty-seven Fernbrook Lane is the exact address."

"Do you even know the president?"

"I know who he is. But seriously, do I look like a kid who knows the president personally?"

"Why do you keep answering my questions with more questions of your own? Like I've said, I've been in a dark crate in the back of a van for the last two days, so there's no way I would know anything more than you. I mean, about my current whereabouts. Though I'm quite sure I know more about everything else than you."

Okay, now, here's where I draw the line in the sand. You can pick on me about my size, my looks, my bad haircuts, the fact that my ears may be weirdly small, the fact that I'm sick all the time, and that I happen to fall down way more than the average kid. But the one thing you can't say about me is that I'm not smart. Because that's the main thing, or perhaps the only thing, I have going for me. Well, besides my stupendous personality and awesome sense of humor. I also happen to have very straight teeth like the twins, so no braces for me.

"I'm plenty smart. And if we're going to be pointing fingers, or paws, or giant furry feet, I'd suggest you point them at yourself, because if you can't tell that this is not the White House, then you're the one who might not be that bright."

Parker Elvis Pembroke IV stared down at me. I'm pretty sure he would have rolled his eyes, if dogs could actually do such a thing.

"Perhaps we should start over. Clearly, we've gotten off on the wrong paw, you and I. Good afternoon, my name is Parker Elvis Pembroke IV. I was born on a farm in Tennessee and have been trained for the last two years to be the president of the United States's new dog. Obviously, as this is not the White House and you are not in any way related to the president, I have been delivered to the wrong address."

"Sheesh, was that so hard? Why couldn't you have said all that from the very beginning and saved us a lot of grief? Seriously—wait one freaky-deaky second here. Did you just say you're the president's dog? As in the president of the United States of America's dog? Are you a Secret Service dog? Do you have those special titanium teeth that can bite through metal? Are you bionic? Can you fly Air Force One?"

"What? No. I have the same teeth I was born with." He flashed them at me. They were big and very white. So the one thing I had in common with him was we both had good teeth. "I'm not a protective dog, though I'd throw myself in front of a bullet if I had to do so to protect my master. But I would do that even if he weren't the president. And protecting our country is just a bonus of patriotic pride. And no, I can't fly Air Force One, but that's because I don't have thumbs, not because I don't know how. I'm sure I could learn to fly Air Force One if I had to do it under extenuating circumstances."

"So then you're just supposed to be the president's regular dog?"

"First off, there is nothing regular about me. Second off, even if I happened to be a regular dog, just by virtue of the fact that I was the president's dog, I would no longer be regular, but instead I would be special. I am the president's personal dog. He picked me out himself twenty-two months ago when I was an eleven-month-old puppy, and I've been in training ever since. I am honed and ready to take my place in history beside him. You see, I'm what you would call an extraordinary dog who is destined to live an extraordinary life."

Well, one thing I knew for sure was that he wasn't lying when he said that. He certainly was extraordinary, as in extraordinarily full of himself. I mean, who goes around saying that he's extraordinary? I mean, even if I was extraordinary in some way, I don't think I'd go around announcing it. I wondered if all dogs were this confident. I also found it interesting that he thought of himself as special too. But when he said he was special, he acted like it was a good thing. You know, I just decided that in my next life, I want to come back as a dog. Of course, knowing my luck, I'd come back as a pound puppy.

Normally, I wouldn't believe such a wackadoo story, but there was something in his tone that made me almost believe him. He sounded so serious. Besides, it was a pretty crazy story once you thought about it.

"Okay, so you're the president's dog. Congratulations to you."

"Thank you. I am very pleased myself. Now, is Benji short for something?"

"Yes, it's short for Benjamin, but no one calls me Benjamin except the principal of my school and my grandmother. I prefer Benji. Like the dog. Hey, that's pretty funny. I have a dog's name and you have a person's name. It's kind of ironic, isn't it?"

"Actually, it's not ironic, it's merely an interesting turn of events. A mere coincidence, as they say. One of my biggest pet peeves is when humans use the word 'ironic' incorrectly. The English language is something to be treasured and appreciated, Benjamin."

"Whatever you say, Elvis."

"Touché."

"What does that mean?"

"It's a French word that means . . . oh, never you mind. It's not important. You see, I'm trying to work on my French, because next week at the White House they are entertaining the French prime minister and his family. They're going to have a big party, and I will be in attendance. So I've naturally been brushing up on my French. It's a beautiful language, if I do say so myself. And here's an interesting tidbit. The French love their dogs. They are even allowed to bring them into restaurants. Have you ever been to France?"

I shook my head. "I like French fries, though."

"Yes, they are quite delicious. But here's another interesting fact. French fries originated in Belgium, not France. But Belgian fries doesn't sound quite the same. Now, perhaps it's time to go straighten out this whole unfortunate turn of events."

"Okay, I guess I'll go tell my mom about the mix-up?"

"Are you asking me or telling me? Because what you said was a statement, but then you added a question mark to it at the end."

This dog was one big hairy piece of work. Good luck, Mr. President.

"I guess I'm telling you."

"Just by adding the words 'I guess' in front of your statement, you are still making it into a question. You should be more assertive in your manner."

If he was going to get annoyed with everything I said, I wasn't going to say anything. We looked at each other silently for a moment. He then stood up and gently nudged me with his giant moist black nose.

"Ahem, are you expecting me to go with you? I'm

actually a little tired from my travels, so I think I'll wait here and rest a bit. I'm sure if you tell your mother to phone the White House, they'll handle the whole matter straightaway."

"Fine." I started toward the kitchen, but then I stopped and turned around. "Do you want any water? Or a cookie?"

Just because he was being rude to me didn't mean I had to stoop to his level. My mom raised me to be a polite host, no matter what the circumstances. I'd probably be cranky if I'd had to ride in a cage for two days too.

"A water and a cookie sounds delightful. Chilled and flat if possible. Thank you, Benjamin. It's very kind of you to offer."

"Aren't all cookies flat?"

"Pardon me?"

"You said you wanted a flat cookie, and I was saying, aren't cookies flat?"

"I was talking about the water, flat, not bubbly. Bubbly water makes me sneeze."

I was about to open my mouth to respond, but I decided this was one conversation that had already gone on long enough. I headed to the kitchen, where my mom was sitting at the kitchen table, talking on the phone while eating a pudding cup.

"Mom. Hey, Mom. Mom. Yoo-hoo, Mom. Mom? Mom! Mooooommmmm!"

"Benji, I'm on the phone! Shhhhhh."

"Sorry, but this is important. It's about the dog."

"Did he pee on my carpet?"

"No. But I need to talk to you about him."

"What is it?"

"We did get the wrong dog. And you're never going to believe this, but the dog we got belongs to the president."

"What are you talking about? What president?"

"The president of the United States."

"Benji, what on earth are you saying? I don't have time for jokes. I'm on the phone. Of course, I've been on hold for the last five minutes."

"Mom, I'm telling you they sent us the wrong dog by mistake, because the dog we have, you know, the enormous black one that is in our living room, he's the president's dog. You know, as in the president of the United States of America's dog."

"How do you know?"

"The dog told me."

"What?"

"The dog. He just told me he's the president's new dog. Anyway, I'm glad he's not mine, because he's kind of snooty when he talks. Hey, did you know that French fries came from Belgium and not France?"

My mom dropped the phone. As I reached over to pick it up for her, she scooped me up in her arms and ran around the kitchen, grabbing her purse and looking for her keys. I had no idea what was happening. The first thing that popped into my head was earthquake, tornado, or hurricane. I'm not sure why, but I'm just telling you what I was thinking, because honestly, why else would she pick me up and throw me over her shoulder if it wasn't some sort of major emergency? I hear forest animals can sense when big danger is coming, like a fire, even from miles and miles away, and they have the instinct to run. So if my mom really was a mama bear in a former life, then it makes sense that she would have this skill too. Her yelling caused Parker Elvis Pembroke to run into the kitchen, which only made her scream again, and right in my ear, because he startled her when he came galloping into the kitchen.

"Oh, well, I guess you should come too," she said to Elvis.

He barked in response, and I immediately wondered why he didn't talk to her like he talked to me. Soon we were in my mom's SUV, driving really fast.

She was breaking every speed limit.

"Mom, hey, Mom. Mom. Yoo-hoo, Mom. Mom? Mom! Mooooommmmm! What's going on? Where are we going?"

"We're going to the emergency room."

"What's wrong? Are you sick? Do you not feel well?" I was scared. As much as I'm not a fan of being sick myself, the thought of something wrong with my mom terrified me. She never got sick. I don't even remember her ever getting a cold. My theory is that germs want to stay on her good side. Here's the deal with my mom. You always want her on your team. The twins didn't get their killer competitive streaks from my dad, that's for sure.

She didn't answer me, but just seeing her white knuckles on the steering wheel made me sit back, close my eyes, and try to take a few deep breaths. Whenever my mom is this stressed, I get stressed, which brings on either one of my fainting spells, or worse, an asthma attack.

Meanwhile, Elvis just sat quietly in the seat next to me. He was so tall, his head touched the roof of the car.

"Benjamin, are you okay? Are you feeling like you're going to faint again?" When he asked, his tone was actually the nicest it had been since he'd arrived.

"Why is he whining like that?" my mother yelled again. "Oh my God, is something happening? What's happening? Is he trying to tell us something? Do something, you dumb dog!"

"I don't know what's going on," I whispered to Elvis. "We're going to the hospital. I think my mom is sick."

"Why do you think she's sick? I believe she thinks you're sick, which is why she's acting so erratic. I'm actually impressed with her driving skills, except for the fact that she keeps running stop signs. She seems to be under great duress."

"Duress? What's that mean? Hey, do you think you could talk on a ten-year-old-kid level versus a president-of-the-United-States level?"

"Fine. Duress means she's under stress or strain."

"Well, I don't need you to tell me that. I've got eyes, you know. Plus she's my mom."

He leaned over and licked my face again, his giant pink tongue slobbering all over me.

"Uchhhhh, what was that for?"

"I wanted to see if you had a fever. You don't."

"Why don't you lick her? I'm fine. She's the one duressing everywhere. Maybe she's the one with a fever. Maybe she's got meningitis?"

Suddenly we screeched to a halt, and Parker Elvis Pembroke was caught off guard. He smashed his face into the back of the front seat. His front paws slid off the seat and onto the floorboard. I tried to disguise my laughter with fake coughing.

I looked out the window and saw that we were parked right by the emergency room. Wow, she never does this, I thought. It must be serious. She usually parks on level B and then thinks she parked on level C, and then we walk around the parking garage with her muttering under her breath for about twenty minutes or so. Anyway, so she jumped out of the car, and so did I, but I was on the other side of the car. She ran around the car toward me and picked me up in her arms like I weighed twenty pounds.

"Hello, people, we've got an emergency here! Help us!" she yelled.

**Dr. Helen walked into** a small, curtained-off section of the ER that barely fit the gurney, my mom, and Elvis (okay, it didn't actually fit Elvis, because his giant furry tail went under the curtain into the next section). She looked at me to make sure I was all in one piece and wasn't covered in blood,

then looked at my mom, who was clutching two empty candy bar wrappers. Then she looked at Elvis; then she looked back at my mom and opened her mouth to speak, but before any words came out of her mouth, she turned her head to look back at Elvis again. He's a dog who's totally worth a double take.

"Now who is this handsome big fellow?" she asked, leaning down to pet Elvis.

"His name is Parker Elvis Pembroke IV, but I'm calling him Elvis."

Parker Elvis Pembroke IV shot me a warning look, but what could he do when my mom was so close by? "Come on," I whispered to him. "Elvis is the coolest name ever."

Dr. Helen stood back up. She looked at my mom's face again, and I guess she's been a doctor long enough to just know what needs to be done in the most efficient way possible.

"Nadine, why don't you take this big guy on a tour of the hospital grounds? I think there are a few trees out there he could easily make his own."

My mom was about to object, but out of all the people in the world, she really trusts Dr. Helen. She grabbed Elvis's leash and they walked out, leaving me alone with Dr. Helen. I took a deep breath, because I was suddenly nervous and my mouth was dry.

"Benji, what's going on?"

I will admit I thought about lying to Dr. Helen because it just seemed so much easier, but as she was literally the very first person to ever see me, like ever, since she was the doctor who delivered me and saved my life, it seemed extra wrong to not tell her the truth.

"I don't really know exactly what's going on, Dr. Helen, but if I had to guess, I think my mom freaked out because I told her that Elvis talks, or rather he talks and I can understand him. I know it sounds weird, but I swear I'm not making it up. He arrived at the house, and when my mom was in the kitchen, he walked around smelling our living room. I introduced myself, and then he introduced himself. By talking. Out loud. To me. And that's not even the craziest part of the story."

Dr. Helen's expression was hard to read, but then again, it's always hard to read. She did lean in slightly when I said that the talking-dog part wasn't the craziest part.

"Well, please continue."

"The dog told me he actually belongs to the president of the United States. There was a mix-up, and he got delivered to my house by mistake."

Okay, now that I'd said it out loud, I absolutely understood why my mom thought I was a total crazy-pants. It was such an outrageous story. I mean, it's one thing to have a talking dog, but a talking dog that belongs to the president of the United States, I mean, really? No wonder my mom freaked out and drove me straight to the hospital.

Dr. Helen then did something that she has never ever done before. She walked over to the gurney, sat down next to me, and put her arm around me.

"Here's the thing about the brain, Benji. It's a very complex and amazing organ, and even though we know a lot about it, there's still a great deal we don't know about it too. And sometimes, when a person experiences head trauma, which you did the other day during your episode, there can be some residual swelling. It can take a while to go down. Sometimes this swelling puts pressure on the brain, and it's that pressure that causes the brain to react in all sorts of ways. Some people just have headaches, but some people see things that aren't there, or have double vision. So it's totally possible this is what's happening with you and your dog. And we could also factor in that you might be a little lonely and in need of a friend too. You've had an awful lot going on in your life for someone your age."

"Dr. Helen, are you trying to tell me I'm a lonely kid, and you think I'm making this all up? I know lots of kids have imaginary friends, and I did too, but Mr. Bobo and Ms. Lingling moved away when I was four to open a restaurant in Arizona. So this is not the same thing at all. I'm telling you, Elvis talked to me in the same way you and I are talking right now. So if you don't believe me, just say it."

"Benji, I'm not saying that at all. What I am saying is when it comes to the brain, I'm a doctor, and I believe anything is possible. And I have read about all sorts of cases where people have head trauma and do amazing things. I've also read a lot about the incredible relationships between owners and their dogs, where they communicate with one another."

"So you're saying you've had other patients who said their dogs talked to them?" Boy, was I relieved.

"No, I wouldn't say that. But there is a first time for everything. Now, here's what we're going to do. As long as Elvis isn't telling you to do anything odd, like jump off a bridge, or that you can fly, I'm not going to worry about it. But here's my advice, which you should take because I'm older and wiser and have multiple graduate degrees framed and hanging on my wall. I know if I had a talking dog, I'd be careful who I shared that information with, if you catch my drift."

"So you believe me?"

"I believe you; I believe in you, but what I don't believe is how big that dog is. You do realize his poops are going to be bigger than you, right?"

"Ewwwww, Dr. Helen. That's so gross." Then I got serious again. "So what do we do about Mom?"

Dr. Helen said she'd take care of my mom, but that she was going to have me stay in the hospital overnight for one more test, to be totally sure nothing was going on with my brain.

"And if I recall correctly, you're getting the tenth punch on your Dino punch card. His shift starts in another few hours."

"That's right!" I was excited now. "I wonder what my prize will be. I hope it's something good."

She smiled and shrugged and said she was pretty sure Dino wouldn't disappoint me.

"Hey, Dr. Helen, do you think Elvis is telling the truth? About him being the president's dog? Or do you think I have the one talking dog who is also a big fat liar?"

"Don't you worry—I'm sure your mom will get to the bottom of the whole dog situation, and if she can't find any answers, she can call me and I'd be happy to email Action Jaxin to see if he could help us. In the meantime, just focus on the positive, which is you don't have to wear the helmet as long as he's here. I personally get a very good vibe from him."

There weren't any private rooms left in pediatrics, so Dr. Helen put us on the fourth floor, which was a mixed bag of patients. I've been on pretty much every floor of the hospital—well, except the subbasement floor, but that's the morgue, and you don't want to get assigned there, because you'd be dead, and that'd be a huge bummer. Normally it's a big deal to get a private room, but Dr. Helen calls in some favors, and a regular shared room is too small for us, mainly because my mom takes up a lot of space with her big personality, and she always insists on spending the night on a cot next to me whenever I have to sleep over. And now that we also had to share the room with a giant dog, we were definitely never going to fit in a regular room.

My mom keeps a duffel bag of stuff in the trunk of her car that she uses to *schjuzz* every room I stay in. She puts up two framed pictures with command tape on the wall. One of them is our family portrait from three years ago, and it's one of my favorite pictures, because every single person in the photo is looking somewhere different than at the camera. I was looking up because the twins told me they just saw a bald eagle (they were lying). My dad was looking down at the ground, my mom was looking at me, and one of the twins was looking right and the other one was looking left. Obviously, this isn't the picture we used for our Christmas card that year, but when I saw it, it made me laugh really hard. I feel like it says a lot about our family. We're a family, but we're all totally different. Anyway, my mom enlarged and framed the picture for me, and she puts it up for me whenever I'm away from home. She also has a sticker of a fake window looking out on a sunny day, and she puts up these curtains around the sticker window.

She says it's too depressing to be in a windowless room. It's all kind of silly, and totally unnecessary, especially for such a short overnight stay, but I don't mind telling you I like that she does it. Because I've spent so much time at this hospital that it sort of feels like my very own room in my home away from home. Anyway, she was just done putting the final touches on my room when we were called to radiology.

You find all types in the radiology waiting room. CT scans are big machines, and you can get a scan of any and all parts of your body. You can even get your whole body scanned. As this was not my first time at the rodeo, I knew the drill, so I wasn't too nervous. Now, how it works in a hospital is they do the most important cases first, and obviously my case was not an emergency, so we were in for a long wait. When my mom looked at her watch for the zillionth time, I got a little curious, and then I figured it out.

"Hey, Mom, don't you have book club tonight?" I asked. My mom loves book club.

"What? Oh, yeah, I guess so. But that's okay."

"What book did you read?"

"We were supposed to read *Anna Karenina* by Leo Tolstoy, but I didn't finish it. Why Marge Rosenfeld had to pick a thousand-page book I'll never know. But I have the CliffsNotes in my purse."

"Mom, isn't the whole point of book club to actually read the book?"

"Benji, book club isn't about the book. It's about women getting together to talk about our lives with an assortment of baked goods nearby. And wine. But don't you worry, it's okay if I skip one."

"What are you talking about? You can't miss book club. You never miss book club. You started book club, and remember how you told everyone that the key to a successful book club is to never miss?"

"We'll see, maybe I'll go, but if I do, I'll come back right afterward."

"Mom, you don't have to come back after book club. I'll see you in the morning."

"You don't want me to come back? At all?"

My mom stared at the dog and then stared back at me. I couldn't tell exactly what was going on in her head, but it didn't seem good. She walked over and patted Elvis on the head.

"What about Elvis?" she asked. "He's going to need something for dinner, and someone has to walk him."

"Mom, I wasn't going to let him starve, plus didn't you say you fed him three bags of Doritos from the cafeteria?"

"I didn't offer him three bags—he actually grabbed three bags on his own and put them by me at the register when I was getting my coffee. It really was quite remarkable."

"Mom, just go. I'll be fine. Dino will help me with Elvis. I've stayed at the hospital a million times. Besides, it's almost six, and Dino will be here soon. And it's my tenth punch, so I'll get a prize. I'll page him, I promise."

I was about to push my mom out, when the waiting room door opened and out came Taisy McDonald, followed by her dad. After I'd run into her two weeks ago, I'd looked her up online and read the *Sports Illustrated* magazine article about her. I learned a lot in that article, mainly that it's not all that surprising how good she is in sports. Not only is her dad Big Tate McDonald, but Taisy's mom was a college basketball superstar. She helped the United States win an Olympic gold medal twenty years ago.

Big Tate led Taisy to a seat and went back into the office, leaving her alone in the waiting room. She didn't look very happy. Since she was at radiology again, it probably meant she hadn't told her dad the truth about her elbow. It was weird to run into her again at the hospital, and I wondered why I couldn't ever run into her somewhere fun like SuperDuperScooper. But I have to say I was still pretty excited. This was probably the first bit of good luck I'd had since losing my lucky titanium lug nut. I would've said the dog was my first bit of good luck, but the jury was still out about how that was going to work.

"Doesn't that little girl over there go to your school?" My mom nudged me.

"Little? She's hardly little. She's probably almost as tall as you are!"

"Why don't you go say hi?"

"What? No way. Mom, no, she barely knows who I

am. I've only talked to her once before. Plus she saw me in my helmet, so I kinda wish she never saw me at all. I mean, of all the people to have to see me in that thing, why did it have to be Taisy McDonald?"

"Wait, why do I know her name?"

"Probably because she's in the paper all the time."

"Oh, is she the star athlete girl?"

"Yup, that's her all right. Her mom is an Olympic gold medalist, and her dad was a football player."

"If she's in your class, of course she knows who you are."

"Mom, she does know who I am, but this is a hospital, not a playground. So let's not cause a scene, okay? Please don't do this."

"Do what? What am I doing?"

Uh-oh, this was breaking bad, and fast. The more you disagree with my mom, the louder she gets. There was no way around it. My mother was going to embarrass me. And as if on cue, Taisy looked up and turned her head in our direction. My mom smiled and waved at her like our house was on fire and she was waving over the fire trucks. Now I had no choice, so I waved at her too. Elvis, not wanting to miss anything, sat up and looked over at Taisy too. You're not going to believe this, and I say this because I barely believed it, but Elvis picked up his paw and did a wave too. I was about to point it out to my mom, but then I thought it was best to keep these things to myself.

Taisy's eyes grew big. A huge smile took over her entire face, and she returned our waves with the biggest wave ever. It was like she used her entire arm. It was by far the warmest, happiest greeting I've ever seen. Of course, I soon found out that expression on her face wasn't for me. It was for Elvis. Some dogs have all the luck. With her superlong legs, Taisy crossed the room in two seconds.

"Who is this puppadooberry cutie? Wow! I love him. He's so big and fuzzy. What's his name?"

"This is Parker Elvis Pembroke IV, but I call him Elvis." My mom elbowed me, and I glared. "And this is my mom. I call her . . . Mom, actually."

Taisy laughed. "Still funny, I see. Nice to meet you, Benji's mom." She shook my mom's hand, which I'm sure my mom loved. She's big on good manners.

Of course, when it comes to manners, my mom wants everyone else to have them, but when it comes to her, there are clearly no rules or boundaries. Instead of just shaking her hand like a normal person, my mom pulled Taisy in for a big, warm hug.

"Hi, Taisy, it's so wonderful to meet you. I love

meeting all my baby Benji's friends."

Taisy took the whole hug thing much better than I did. In fact, I was freaking out just watching it. I didn't know what would ruin my life more, my mom hugging her or the fact that my mom had just called me "baby" in front of Taisy McDonald! Before I could say anything, Taisy hugged Elvis.

"Parker Elvis Pembroke IV, what a great name. Aren't you a cutie-wootie? Aren't you the furriest bestest baby in da whole wide world? Who's da baby? You are. You are."

And again she buried her face in his neck fur. Elvis clearly enjoyed the attention, because his tail wagged so hard it kept whacking me on the leg and created enough of a breeze to make my hair move.

"Look at you. Who's got a big head? Who's got the biggest, cutest head in the whole world? Huh? You are the handsomest doggy ever. You are, yes, you are. Oh you are so lucky, Benj."

She'd called me Benj again! No one calls me Benj, but when she says it, I always feel like I've had been Benj my whole life. My mom elbowed me and raised her eyebrows. I knew she wanted me to say something back, but I glared at her to stop pushing! In a million years, I never expected to hear Taisy McDonald baby-talking to a dog, let alone calling me Benj. This was a completely different Taisy from the girl I'd talked to two weeks ago.

"So, what brings you to the radiology department?" I said. Okay, so out of everything I could have possibly said, that was probably the stupidest thing I could have said.

"I had to get a scan of my elbow."

My mom was in there before I could even reply. "Oh no, honey, that's too bad. I'm sure it will be fine soon. I know how scary that must be for you, because you're such an amazing athlete. Benji's older brothers play sports too."

"Oh, thank you. But don't worry, I'm sure it'll be fine. My dad always goes a little overboard about these things."

"I know it seems that way, but he only does it because he loves you so much."

I could tell my mom was stressing Taisy out, so I felt like I had to get in there to save her.

"So Taisy, don't you feel like those big MRI machines kinda look like giant bread machines? What's your favorite kind of bread?"

Taisy and my mom gave me a weird look. I shrugged. I don't know why I said it either. I just opened my mouth and it came out. But it is totally true. Those machines look and sound like bread machines. I always feel like a piece of dough going in there.

"Uh, I guess my favorite bread is raisin walnut bread."

"Mine too. I mean, except for the walnuts. If I ate a walnut, I could die. But raisins and me? We're tight." I crossed my fingers for emphasis. "Yeah, some of my best friends are raisins." Whoa, why couldn't I shut up?

"Benji has a nut allergy." My mom tried to help me out of the hole I was clearly busy digging for myself.

Taisy was totally unfazed. "So how is it that I didn't know you had such a supercool dog?"

"Oh, that's because he's new. I just got him. Like, today. He's my new therapy dog. I got him so I don't have to wear that helmet anymore."

"Really? That's awesome. He's the best dog I've ever seen. Well, besides my dog, Princess Daisy, but since she's not here, I can tell you right now your dog is just as cute. I love dogs. I wish I could get a second one, but my dad says one is enough. And with all my practicing, I barely get to see my one dog enough as it is."

"Taisy, hon. We need to go." Taisy's dad came out from the back, calling her from the other side of the waiting room. He had a really deep voice, kind of like thunder. Taisy stood up, but not before kissing Elvis all over his face.

"Coming, Dad. I was just saying hi to my friend Benj." Taisy turned to me. "Well, I guess I'll see you at school later this week?"

I didn't even hear what she said, mainly because I was still in shock that she had called me her friend Benj, to her dad. That meant an actual real-life sports hero with two Super Bowl rings knew that his daughter had a friend named Benj. My mom nudged me to answer.

"What? Sorry, what did you say?"

"Will you be at school tomorrow?"

"Probably not tomorrow, but definitely the day after."

Okay, I really wanted to call her Tais, like how she called me Benj, but by the time I decided to go for it, they were already gone. As soon as the door closed, I whipped around and faced my mom.

"Mom, we need to have a little talk. You know I don't like you calling me 'baby' period, but you can *never ever ever* call me 'baby' in front of other people, okay?"

"You're overreacting! I'm sure Taisy's dad calls her 'baby' too."

"I don't care what Taisy's dad calls her. I only care what you call me in front of Taisy, okay?"

"Why, do you like Taisy?"

"Mom! Stop! Forget I said anything."

Talk about being saved by the bell. The nurse called out my name.

"Okay, I'm going to go, but I'm definitely going to come back. I don't want my baby to be alone."

"I. Am. Not. Your. Baby! I can take care of myself. Well, I mean, for a night I can. You know what I mean. And speaking of that, I wanted to let you know that I've decided I'm old enough to stay overnight here on my own. Like starting tonight."

"First off, you are, and you will always will be, my baby. Even when you're twenty-five, you're still going to be my baby, and you know it. And if you don't want me to stay overnight, I guess I don't have to." My mom sounded brave, but I could tell I'd hurt her feelings a little. "And today is your first day with Elvis, and maybe you need help. I mean, do we really know if he's able to care for you properly?"

Elvis answered my mom with a short bark. My mom startled and looked at him.

"How strange. It's as if he understood I was talking about him."

"Well, you did say his name, and dogs like these can probably read the tone of your voice. Maybe he can tell you're not happy. Mom, I'm sorry if I—"

"Don't say another word. I understand."

I sighed. She was doing that rapid blinking thing she does when she's trying not to cry. My mom says all emotionally intelligent people are criers, and that it's actually good for you. But when she is trying not to cry in public, she blinks. Then her top lip starts to quiver, and then if she starts fanning her eyes, it's all over. But sometimes she gets it all under control with the blinking. Today, lucky for me, was one of those days. It's not that I didn't want her to stay. I love my mom more than anyone and anything in the entire world. I just wanted a little space. She needed one more nudge, but a gentle one this time.

"C'mon, Mom. Go have fun at your book club talking about Anna Can-ya-pass-me-some-more-cake-'cause-I-didn't-read-the-book."

She laughed. "It's *Anna Karenina*, and I read the first chapter."

"Mom, it's nothing personal, but tonight's my tenth punch on my punch card and Dino is going to get me a surprise, and I'm just afraid if you're here he might, you know."

"What, what do I know?"

"Mom, he might not do anything all that fun, because he'll be too afraid of you. Please, Mom, I want to stay alone. I mean, with Elvis. I'll pretend it's a sleepover."

My mom made a face when I said this. I'd struck a chord with her, because she always tells me that when she was younger, her favorite thing was slumber parties, and we both knew I'd never been invited to one.

Well, that clinched the deal. She stood up to leave and gave me a huge hug. "Mom, can't breathe. I'll see you tomorrow. It's just one night."

She nodded and quickly walked to the door. At the doorway, she turned around and blew me a kiss. I smiled and said good-bye. She blew me another kiss, and then another, and then another, until I pretended to catch one in my hand and smush it on my cheek. This is what we used to do a million years ago, when I was a little kid and she had finished tucking me into bed. It felt silly doing that at ten years old. But it made her happy, so I did it.

# 7

When Dino works the night shift, he takes his lunch break around three or four in the morning. I was hoping he'd show up and give me my surprise then. I slept on and off, but it's not so easy to sleep in a hospital. You hear lots of voices and banging from the hallway, and nurses wake you every few hours to take your temperature and blood pressure. So I was half asleep when the first paper airplane sailed into the room. I didn't even see it. But Elvis, who was asleep on the floor next to me, sat up suddenly.

"What was that?" he asked. His tone of voice was very serious.

"What was what?" I mumbled, sitting up.

"I heard something. Shhhhhh."

"I didn't hear an—"

"Shhhhhhhh!"

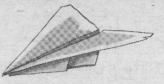

Okay, no one likes getting shushed in general. But getting shushed by your own dog? Even more annoying.

And right then, another paper airplane sailed into the room. This time I saw it against the mermaid nightlight my mom always puts in my rooms. (Apparently, when I was really small and we were on some beachy vacation, I saw it in a gift shop and pointed at it and said, "Mama." The mermaid has big blond hair like my mom's. So she bought it and made up stories about how she used to be a mermaid in a past life.) I reached up to grab it when Elvis said, "Stop! Don't touch it!" The tone of his voice was so stern, I pulled my hand back in. Elvis galloped to the other side of my bed to investigate. I flipped on the lamp, and three more paper airplanes sailed into my room, one after the other.

"There's more! Hey! I bet this is the beginning of my surprise from Dino."

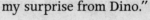

Finally the last plane sailed in, landing perfectly at the foot of my bed. I leaned forward to grab it when a big black paw slapped down on top of it.

"I said don't touch it."

"Elvis, it's fine. Now lift your big fat paw and let me get it. It's a paper airplane, for Pete's sake. What's the worst thing that can happen? I get a paper cut?" Elvis lifted his paw, and I grabbed the now-crumpled plane. The plane had the number 6 written on one wing. On the other wing it said, *Open me last.*

"Quick, we gotta find all the other planes!" I scrambled out of bed and found all the planes except for number three. I looked everywhere until Elvis finally admitted he had caught one in his mouth and spit it out in the trash can. I pulled out the soggy mess, but I couldn't read it because all the ink had blurred.

"I really hope all the important stuff wasn't in that airplane," I said as I laid them all out on the bed.

"I'm not too worried, I've been trained in code cracking."

I rolled my eyes. Of course he'd been trained in code cracking.

Here is what the planes said:

Paper Airplane #1: *Surprise! Congrats on the tenth hole in your punch card!*

Paper Airplane #2: *At exactly 3:33 a.m., go to the*

*far left elevator and push the SB3 button.*

Paper Airplane #3: Blurry mess (thanks to Elvis).

Paper Airplane #4: *Bring a sweatshirt. It might get a little cold.*

Paper Airplane #5: *Try not to get caught leaving your room.*

Paper Airplane #6: *If you get caught, do not tell anyone anything.*

Great, the third paper airplane probably said where we were going to go, I thought. I guessed now it really would be a surprise. It was already 3:27 a.m. I grabbed my sweatshirt and put on my slippers.

"We've got to go now. C'mon!"

"I don't think it's a good idea to roam the hospital at night. You should stay in bed, Benjamin."

"Oh, come on. I'll be fine. I feel great. And Dino's a nurse. What are you? Chicken?"

"Of course not. I have very few fears. Well, I'm not thrilled to be in a thunderstorm, but I'm not scared of it either."

"Then let's go." I made a move toward the door, but Elvis blocked me.

"All I'm saying is you are in the hospital for a reason. Perhaps it's

113

not the best time for an adventure. There are rules of conduct for every situation."

"First off, I'm in the hospital because of you and your big mouth."

"Please, pray tell, how this could possibly be my fault?"

"You're the one who talked, you're the one who told me that wackadoo story about being the president's dog, and then I told my mom, and she thought I was off my rocker, and here we are."

Elvis stared at me. "Fine, I'll take my share of the blame, as perhaps I didn't have to lead with the White House, but still . . ."

"Stop wasting time. Why can't I just have some fun? More importantly, why can't you? You're just a dog, and I thought dogs were supposed to be fun."

"How dare you, sir. You take that back!"

"What? How dare who? I'm sorry. What did I say?"

"I'm not *just* a dog. I'm a purebred, highly educated, superbly skilled dog who is probably smarter than you. Do you know CPR?"

"No. Do you know who all the presidents are?"

"Of course I do. Can you name all the capitals of all the states?"

"Yes. Do you know where Bora-Bora is on a globe?"

"Certainly. Can you tell me the year man first landed on the moon?"

"Duh. Do you know what pi is?"

"Who has pie? I love pie."

"I'm not talking about pie you eat, I'm talking about the number pi. *P-I*. But I like pie too. Banana cream is my favorite. My mom makes a great one."

"Yes, of course I know the number pi. How many digits can you do of pi?"

"3.141592653589. Thirteen. And you?"

"3.141592653589793238462. Twenty-two."

"Show-off." Fine, so maybe he was smarter than me. But why couldn't he ever act like a regular dog? "So can you even do any regular dog tricks? Can you catch a Frisbee?"

"Why on earth would I want to catch a Frisbee? I only do things that I believe will help serve mankind. I hardly think catching Frisbees does anything for the greater good of humanity."

"Can you just talk normally? And I think dogs who catch Frisbees are really talented and lots of fun, so you may want to think about learning how."

"What are you implying by that statement?"

"I'm not implying anything. I'm telling you you're not fun."

"I am too."

"Then let's go have some fun." I started toward the door, stepping around Elvis. "Fine, don't come. See if I care. And besides, according to you, you're not my dog anyway, so it's all good." And with that I popped my head out the door, looking both ways down the hall. The coast was clear, so I made a break for it and ran toward the elevators. Within two seconds Elvis was running by my side. He decided to come after all.

Luckily, we didn't see anyone, but it took a while before the far left elevator showed up. I pressed the down button, but by the time the right elevator came up, it was already 3:35 a.m. We were late. I hate being late. I pressed the SB3 button inside the elevator and noticed my breathing growing rapid and shallow. This is how most of my asthma attacks start. I get nervous, and then I get nervous that I'm getting nervous, and then I really get nervous about getting nervous. Then I take deep breaths so I calm down, but then it doesn't feel like I can get enough air into my lungs and that makes me even more nervous, which is when I take faster short breaths, which can sometimes give me the hiccups, and then . . .

Elvis pushed the red stop button with his nose. The elevator screeched to a halt. I've seen that happen in movies plenty, but I've never been in an elevator where someone did it before, and especially not a dog! Now I was really nervous.

"Benjamin. Everything is okay. You're okay. You need to try to calm down."

"Calm down? Calm down?! We're late and you just stopped the elevator, which is going to make us more late. Oh no, I'm feeling dizzy. Am I sweating? Is it warm in here? I'm gonna faint, aren't I?"

But just before I fainted, Elvis pushed me against the wall and licked my face. Blech, it was so gross and warm and slobbery, but also ticklish on my neck. I laughed, and suddenly I started to feel better again.

"Stop it! Stop it! That tickles."

"Rule number one: Don't leave a room without me and in midconversation. It's rude," Elvis said. "Rule number two: Don't get mad at me when I say I don't think it's a good idea for us to run around the hospital in the middle of the night. Rule number three: Don't tell me I'm not fun. I'm plenty fun. I can tell a knock-knock joke in French, so next week when I'm at my White House party, I'll be a laugh riot. And just in case I'm not being clear, you need to understand something. I'm not with you to be fun, I'm here to do my job, which is to protect you. I spent two years training so I could do my job right. I took and passed every single class at my dog academy. I can lead a blind person. I can detect heart attacks and alert people who are about to have a seizure. I can water rescue. I can get you out of a burning building. I can dig my way out of any yard. If you get lost, I can use smell to find you miles away. I can handle any dangerous situation and get you to safety easily and with confidence. I graduated at the top of my class. No other dog worked harder than me. I take my job very seriously. And when I know you're safe, you and I can chat and bicker and joke around and fight over dumb stuff, but my number-one job is to keep you safe. And yes, you are correct, technically I am not your designated service dog, but until this little mix-up is all cleared up, I strongly feel the honorable thing to do would be to fill in for now. I'm certain it is what the president would expect of me. So, are you feeling better now? Can I restart the elevator?"

I nodded. With that, Elvis walked over to the elevator knob, gently grasped it between his front teeth, and pulled it. The elevator moved again. I didn't say anything. Suddenly, I felt shy around Elvis.

"I get it. And I didn't mean to be rude. I just didn't want to be late."

The elevator stopped at SB3. SB3 stands for sub-basement level three, which was the very bottom of the entire hospital, because there was the basement level, subbasement level two, and then subbasement level three, where the morgue was located.

Wait a second . . . suddenly it all made sense. SB3 was the morgue! Dino was taking me to the morgue! When the doors opened, Dino was standing there with a huge smile on his face.

"No way! Are you . . . ? Are we . . . ? We're not really going to . . . ? I can't believe it!" I said to Dino as.Elvis followed me into the hallway and I stared at a sign that was posted on the wall. It clearly said EGbgee.

"Whoa, is that a dog or a bear?" Dino said as soon as he saw Elvis.

"It's a dog. His name is Elvis."

"Elvis? Whoa, cool name."

"See, I told you it was cool," I said to Elvis.

"Are you talking to the dog?" Dino cocked his head and looked at me.

"The dog's official name is Parker Elvis Pembroke IV, but I call him Elvis. What do you think?"

Dino held out his giant hand for Elvis's giant nose to smell, and then he patted him on his head. Dino talked to Elvis loudly and slowly, kind of the way my mom talks to my dad's mom, who currently lives in a rest home in California.

"Hello, doggie. My name is Dino. You are really big."

"You're one to talk," Elvis barked.

"Hey, I felt like he understood me." Dino smiled. "Too bad neither of us speaks dog so we'd know what he said, right?"

"Oh I doubt he said anything interesting anyway," I said. "Let's go."

"You know, Benji, if you're scared or freaked out, we don't have to do this," Dino said.

I was terrified and really, really freaked out, but I really, *really* wanted to go. I've always been curious about the morgue, and I've seen a dead body or two on television, but I've never seen one in person.

"Are we going to see a dead body?"

Dino knows me well, so he knew my anxiety level was pretty high. He watched me carefully and said that we didn't have to see a dead body if I didn't want to, but that we could at least walk around down there.

"Think of the stories you can tell all your friends at school," he said.

"Yeah, that's for sure."

I said this as though it was true. I didn't want to admit I don't actually have any real friends at school. But there were a few people I could tell, like my mom, and the twins, my dad, Ms. Hensel the librarian, and probably Ms. Blaine, but that might be risky, because she's the type of teacher who'd offer me extra credit if I turned it into a class presentation, "Me and My Trip to the Morgue," a diorama by Benji Wendell Barnsworth. Normally, I'd tell Dino and Dr. Helen my stories, but obviously Dino is part of the story, and I'm betting Dino wouldn't want me sharing this adventure with Dr. Helen, since she was basically his boss. But I have to admit that the very first person who popped into my head when he said that was Taisy McDonald.

"Dino, I didn't know you were Taisy's uncle," I said. "Did you know she's in my class at school?"

"What? Get out of here! You go to Saint Elmo's Street Elementary School?"

"Yup."

"I guess I assumed you were way younger than Taisy. No offense, little man, but she's almost twice your size."

"Just because I'm shorter doesn't mean I'm younger. Spending lots of time in hospitals put my reading level ahead of other kids."

"Taisy's a good girl. My favorite niece is the daughter of my least favorite brother. Go figure, huh?"

I could tell he didn't really want to discuss it anymore, and besides, the morgue probably wasn't the place for idle chitchat about the people we had in common outside of the hospital. I definitely wanted to know more about Taisy, but I'd have to wait.

"Earth to Benji. Come in, come in."

"What? Oh, sorry. I want to do this."

"You're sure?"

"No, but I want to do it anyway."

"Man, I can see the little hairs on the back of your neck standing straight up."

"Dino, I want to do this."

Elvis sensed my nervousness, or perhaps the fact that my teeth were chattering even though I wasn't cold was a giveaway, but he placed his nose under my left arm and tossed his head so that my hand landed on top of his head, making me pet him.

Elvis spoke quietly. "Petting dogs helps people with high blood pressure relax. And Benjamin, you need to relax."

"You gotta keep him quiet," Dino said. "We can't get caught walking around down here. It's bad enough we're down here, but having a dog down here would be worse. Why is he making so much noise?"

"I don't know, but let's hope it's not because he sees dead people." I chuckled nervously at my own joke and petted Elvis like he suggested. His fur was silky smooth, and I had to admit it was working. I felt calmer. I also realized that where I heard Elvis talking, other people seemed to hear him barking or whining.

We walked into a large main room filled with steel drawers like you see on cop shows when they have to go to the morgue. The room was empty, but there were lots of long silver tables. There was also a half-eaten tray of food on one of the tables.

"Ew, if I worked in a morgue, I don't think I'd be bringing my tray back here to eat. Gross."

"So, now that we're here, is there anything you want to do?" Dino asked.

"Do? Like what are my options?"

"I don't know. I figure kids are into creepy things. We could look at a dead body. We could guess which drawers are empty and which ones are full and then open them to see who was right. We could use a Sharpie and you can sign underneath one of these tables and say that Benji Barnsworth was here . . . but not dead."

Dino's ideas were all interesting, but I wasn't sure if any were exactly right. I was pretty excited to be in the morgue. I was much less excited at the thought of seeing a real dead body. The smell down here alone was already starting to make me a little queasy. It smelled like a fake smell that people spray so that it won't smell like actual dead people.

Elvis walked over, cocked his head to one side, and stared at me hard.

"Sorry, but I'm trying to think of something to do down here. It's not every day I get to see a morgue. Who knows when I'll ever be in a morgue again? I mean, when I'm alive and can actually enjoy it a little."

"I'm pretty sure that morgues are not on anyone's top ten lists of fun times, so I think this is pretty much as good as it gets. Seen it, done it, let's go," said Elvis.

He was right about the morgue. All the cool things in a morgue probably involved seeing or touching a dead person, and if I did that now when I was ten, what would I have to look forward to when I was older? I decided that it'd be cool to get a picture of myself down here. Dino told me to hop on up on a table, and he'd take a picture of me playing dead. Now why didn't I think of that brilliant idea?

Dino picked me up and sat me down on a table, which was really cold, by the way, and I played dead. This was going to be the coolest picture ever. Dino took a few, and then I had a brainstorm. I asked Dino if he'd take a few pictures of me and Elvis together.

"Elvis, you get up on this table next to me and play dead too."

"I will do no such thing."

"Please."

"Benjamin, I'm working. Remember our little talk? You apparently have the memory of a fruit fly. I don't like to play games when I'm working, and if I were going to play one, it wouldn't be playing dead."

"I'm playing dead too. It's not like I'm asking you to do anything that I'm not doing. C'mon, it'll be fun, just try it. Hey, Dino, get the camera ready."

"Yo, Benji, maybe he doesn't want to do it. And this table is probably too high for him to jump on, and I'm big and strong, but I'm not sure I'm big and strong enough to lift a two-thousand-pound dog onto a table. It isn't so easy for us big guys to . . ."

This next part I'm going to tell you like it happened in slow motion, even though it didn't. But if this were a movie, this part would definitely be in slow motion, because you'd have to see it that way to believe it.

I hadn't known Elvis all that long, but from what I gathered about his personality, all he had to do was hear someone say that he couldn't do something, like jump up onto an exam table in a morgue, and suddenly there was nothing stopping him from doing it. What I admire is that he's a dog of action and not of words. It's not like he got all flustered and was all, how dare you, and you take that back, and you did not just say that. Nope, Elvis calmly trotted in the other direction, paused, and then ran.

Here's the thing about massive dogs. They run faster than you think, and it's amazing to see all that hair flying. As my mom would say, it's like he was in a dog shampoo commercial. Now, the only thing even more amazing than seeing a dog that big run is seeing a dog that big jump. It's like watching a jumbo 747 plane take off. You just can't imagine that giant hunk of metal flying. With Elvis, when he sprang off his back paws, my brain went into overdrive. I thought, There's no way that giant hunk o' dog is gonna get in the air, but he did. He leaped up. Let me say this, these tables are at least four and a half feet tall. I needed Dino to boost me up onto it, because it was too tall and my arms are too weak. So seeing a dog jump that high was crazy cool.

Our mouths dropped open as he went up in the air. And it was even more dramatic for me, because it almost looked like he was going to land on top of me (which would definitely have crushed me and put me in a morgue drawer for real).

Now here's the catch. These tables were on wheels. And the wheels weren't locked when Elvis landed on the table. The force of a two-hundred-pound dog landing on a table with wheels after a running start propelled the table across the room like a runaway freight train. Dino and I screamed. And a split second later the table slammed into the far wall with a huge crash with Elvis on it. Somehow he still managed to stay on. Dino grabbed me off my table and ran over to check on Elvis.

"Holy moly! That was the most awesome thing I've ever seen! Are you okay?"

Elvis didn't reply. He just rolled onto his back, put his legs up in the air, and flopped his tongue out the side of his mouth, playing dead like a champ. Seriously, I don't think Tom Cruise could have done it any better himself. (My dad is a big Tom Cruise fan. I've seen *Top Gun* with him at least three times, and he's seen it at least ten more times than that. I'm also a big fan of *Mission Impossible*.)

Dino and I howled. We laughed so long and so hard my stomach hurt. It was the funniest thing ever. Dino took a bunch of pictures, and then he showed me what a toe tag is, which is sort of like the little ID tag with your name on it that you put on your backpack. Apparently, when you die, they put a tag like that on your toe so they don't lose you. We found some in a drawer and hung one on Elvis's back paw. The entire time he just lay there and played dead, and after a few minutes I got a little worried.

"You are playing, right?" I whispered.

His tail wagged a little for yes, but he didn't break from his acting scene. He even let me squeeze up on the table next to him, and we both played dead together, though I will say his "dead dog" looked far more impressive than my "dead Benji" pose.

As fun as it was to pose for the pictures, they were even funnier to look at. I begged Dino to make me some copies, but he told me that it was best to delete them all.

"What? But why?"

"Little dude, you may not understand this yet, but you have to trust me. I'm a thousand percent sure you do not want to tell your mom I took you to visit the morgue if you ever want to see me alive again. She would not approve, at all. And because of this, we need to get rid of all the evidence that we were ever down here. Besides, I'm pretty sure we broke all sorts of rules, and if it got back to the head of the hospital that a dog was down here, well, let's just say I could end up with a tag on my toe for real. Understand?"

"I guess so. But couldn't we just keep one or two?"

"Nope. I've learned that some things are best left as good memories. I don't want to lose my phone and have these pictures end up on the national nightly news."

"But you'd be famous."

"Maybe so, but I'd rather be famous for something cool I do as opposed to being murdered by your mom. I'm just saying, you never know what could happen. And it's better for all of us that we just enjoy them and then get rid of the evidence. Trust me. Okay?"

"But these are the first pictures I ever took with Elvis."

"And where's he going? You can take more pictures with him later. C'mon, it's not like your mom won't be taking a million pictures of you and your new giant dog."

"True." Dino has actually seen quite a few of my mom's scrapbooks about me. His favorite series of pictures is "Benji's First Time Canoeing," which shows me getting into a canoe, trying to paddle a canoe, losing the first paddle, losing the back-up paddle, trying to reach the paddle, and then finally flipping over the canoe. So there was no doubt there would soon be a leather-bound book labeled "Benji's First Dog."

Besides, the last thing I wanted was for Dino to get in trouble because of me, and as I was having the best day of my entire life, I didn't want something bad to happen later to ruin the memory. We looked at every single picture one more time, and then he deleted them one by one.

I'm telling you, it was hands down the absolute most fun I've ever had in a morgue. Ever. When I got back to my room, I had a hard time falling asleep, mainly because the day had been so full of strange and wonderful things.

"Why aren't you asleep?" Elvis asked me.

It had become weirdly normal to hear a dog talk, but it's not so normal to hear a dog trying to whisper.

"How do you know I'm not asleep?"

"I can tell by your breathing, first off, and secondly you just confirmed it by answering my question."

"I don't know—why aren't you asleep?"

"I don't know, but I could sleep if I wanted to sleep. I was waiting for you to fall asleep. And I was thinking about Taisy."

"What about her?"

"Just that she reminds me of the daughter of Action Jaxin, my favorite trainer on the farm."

"Are you talking about Lola Beth, the girl who was born premature like me?"

Elvis was surprised that I remembered her, but I explained I didn't know much, only that Dr. Helen saved her life when she was a baby the same way she saved mine. Elvis said that Lola Beth had some learning disabilities and had a very hard time learning to read.

One of her therapists suggested she should try reading to a dog, because that would offer her a sense of purpose but at the same time she didn't have to worry about the dog judging her if she made any mistakes.

"I consider myself really lucky that out of the one hundred or so dogs on the farm, she picked me. It was great. Sometimes she'd fall asleep at night reading to me, so I got to sleep on her bed instead of going back out to the barn to sleep in my pen. She's the reason I know so much, because once she got better at reading, she wanted to read anything and everything. Anyway, Taisy and Lola Beth have a lot in common. They're both warm and sweet. But Taisy is much, much taller."

"Taisy is much much taller than everyone," I responded.

"Yeah, I like her. It makes sense that she's related to Dino. They're both so friendly. Technically, I'm not supposed to let anyone hug, pet, kiss, or baby-talk me when I'm working, but . . ."

"But she's so irresistible, you kind of can't help it?"

"Yes, that seems to be the issue at hand."

"Well, seeing that you're not technically even my dog, then while you're here helping me out temporarily, I think we could let some things slide."

"How kind of you. But I want you to understand

I have all the training of a regular service dog, so you can fully count on me in the event of an emergency."

"You mean to say if the school was on fire, you'd make sure to rescue me?"

"Absolutely. Right after I rescued Taisy."

I burst out laughing. Elvis had finally made a joke. Well, he finally made a funny joke. "Good one, Elvis. Look, I like Taisy too. But I don't know her very well."

"Isn't she in your class?"

"There are a lot of kids in my class. She's sporty, and if you haven't figured it out, I'm the opposite of sporty. And usually kids hang around other kids who are like them. Also, when you met her, she was totally different than she is at school. She's really intense in school. Everyone high-fives her in the hallways, even the teachers."

"Well, she didn't seem surprised to see you in the waiting room."

"Well, that's just because everyone at school knows that I'm in the hospital a lot."

"How do they know that?"

I didn't really feel like getting into it, but I told him that I'm absent a lot for being sick, and when Ms. Blaine takes attendance and she calls out my name and I don't answer, you kind of can't help but notice. I also told him a little about my "episode" at school. The twins told me that even the junior high kids in their building were talking about it. It's not every day an ambulance shows up with flashing lights and a siren at our school.

"I'm really worried a video of it will appear on You-Tube."

"Well, if it's not there now, it probably won't show up."

"That's not necessarily true. Someone might have caught it on video, but they didn't post it. If there's a video, I'm pretty sure Billy Thompson will track it down and post it if he can."

"Billy Thompson? Who is that?"

"Oh, just this kid in school that I hate."

"Benji, it's not proper to hate people."

"Fine, he's a kid at school who is the bane of my existence and who I intensely dislike so much it makes my stomach hurt."

"Okay, that's much better, and nice usage of the vocabulary word 'bane.' But I wouldn't lose any sleep over this Billy person posting anything on the internet. There's no sense in worrying about things you can't control. Besides, you have a lot of people looking out for you, and if he does something improper like that, I'm sure your Mom will take care of it straight away, which means he's the one who should really be worried. I pride myself on being afraid of very little, but your Mom even makes me a little nervous."

I chuckled at that too. Okay, I'll admit, Elvis could be pretty funny when he wanted to be.

**There are three different** fourth-grade
teachers in my school, and I may be biased, but I
definitely have the best one. Ms. Blaine is fairly new to
the school. So even though she's heard about my older
twin brothers, she doesn't compare me to them like all my
past teachers did. Anyway, as soon as Ms. Blaine met
Elvis, she was all over him, petting him, stroking his
head, scratching his ears, and cooing at him in that

funny way people do when they love animals more than people. I was actually pretty surprised. This was not the same Ms. Blaine I had described to Elvis before we came to school today.

Yesterday, when Elvis and I got home after the hospital, I was exhausted. And even though I kept trying to nap, Elvis asked me all sorts of questions about my school, my teachers, and what he could expect the next day. I finally showed him my third-grade yearbook to shut him up. My mom came into my room to bring us a snack and caught me talking out loud to Elvis. I was trying to explain to him why my hair was so crazy-pants in my class picture last year. It all came down to bad timing on my part, because I had just finished presenting my science report on static electricity, which I had demonstrated by rubbing a balloon on my head, which had caused some of my hair to stand straight up, and then, of course we were called for pictures. Elvis found this story highly amusing.

Anyway, my mom gave me a strange look, and I was about to explain what I was talking about, but I thought about Dr. Helen's advice and decided to keep my mouth shut instead. She didn't press me, which goes to show Dr. Helen was right about how maybe my mom didn't need to know everything. Finally, after eating a plate of banana bread, Elvis fell asleep and, thankfully, so did I.

I wondered if Elvis remembered what I had told him about Ms. Blaine, because this was a totally different Ms. Blaine than I was used to. I just was so shocked watching her swooning over Elvis. Ms. Blaine is fairly strict, in my opinion. She's a no-nonsense New Yorker type who gives off the air that she's heard it all, so it's best to not even bother lying to her. While she was petting Elvis, she told me she has a friend in California who has the exact same type of dog, but female, and she joked that she'd show Elvis a picture of her later. So now my teacher is trying to make a love match for my dog? Or the president's dog? If Elvis found a girlfriend, what would that make her? The First Lady Dog of the White House?

Elvis enjoyed all the attention. Why wouldn't he? Ms. Blaine is by far the prettiest teacher in school. She doesn't dress like the other teachers, in print dresses. She usually wears all black and looks like she belongs in a science fiction movie about the future.

My class has twenty-seven kids in it, and pretty much every pair of eyes was on me, or truthfully, on Elvis, when we walked into my classroom the next morning. Ms. Blaine made Jesse Snyder switch seats with me so I could sit on the aisle and Elvis could lie next to me without blocking anyone. Jesse wasn't happy about it, but he knew better than to object, because Ms. Blaine never puts up with students talking back to her. She's quick to give you extra homework if you choose not to obey her commands. She's always saying, "Here's the deal. I'm the teacher and you're not. So what I say goes. If that's a problem with anyone here, I have plenty of extra homework assignments that I'm happy to pass out." See, very straightforward and simple. No guesswork at all when it comes to what she wants and what her expectations are. We kids have enough on our minds when we're in fourth grade, so it's nice to have an adult in our lives who we don't have to try to figure out.

My new seat was the third chair from the front in the first row on the left by the door. I had only sat down for one second before Ms. Blaine said she wanted me to come up to the front of the classroom and introduce our new special guest. This was the last thing I wanted to do, but like I said, who am I to object to anything Ms. Blaine asks of me?

So I went to the front of the classroom, and Elvis walked up and sat right next to me. Let me be very clear, when Elvis is sitting up next to me, we're pretty much the same height, and of course, he weighs about four times what I do, so we looked like quite an unlikely pair.

"Hi, everyone. This is my new service dog, Elvis. Well, his full name is Parker Elvis Pembroke IV."

Immediately the class started laughing. I wasn't sure why, but I looked over at Ms. Blaine, who motioned me to continue.

"He prefers his full name, but I think he looks more like an Elvis. He's a Newfoundland, which means he's in the working class of dog breeds. Newfoundland is in Canada, and it's very cold there. These dogs are used for water rescue. They were taken on ships so they could save sailors who went overboard. So I'm assuming he can swim, but I haven't seen him swim, so I don't know for sure."

"Of course I can swim." Elvis barked twice.

"Oh yeah, he can swim." The class found this very amusing, that I was pretending to understand what my dog had to say.

"Very good, Benji. Now can you tell us why you have him?"

"Well, first off, there's been a mix-up from the farm where we got him, so there's a chance he's not even my permanent dog. My mom has been calling the place, but the guy she's supposed to talk to is on vacation at an eco lodge in South America. Apparently eco lodges don't have very good cell phone reception, because her calls keep going straight to voicemail. I suppose no one wants to hear about him, though."

Again the classroom broke out into laughter, which was weird, because I wasn't trying to be funny or anything.

"So Benji, can you tell us why you need a service dog?"

"Sure, Ms. Blaine. I need a service dog because a few weeks ago I had a seizure in the hallway, which I'm sure everyone has heard about. And my doctor isn't totally sure yet what caused it and whether I might have another one. She wanted me to wear the world's ugliest helmet, but instead I got the world's largest dog. Elvis has been trained to help me if it happens again."

Ms. Blaine raised her hand, which I found a little odd, but I went with it.

"Yes, Ms. Blaine, did you have a question?"

"I did, Benji, thank you. What exactly will Elvis do if it happens again? I mean, what sort of training did he have to be a service dog?"

"That's a very good question, but I have to be honest and say I don't really know the answer. My mom says that dogs who have this sort of training are able to sense it before I have a seizure, and then they make sure I'm in a safe location in case I fall down. They also know how to call for help. Just this morning when I tripped and fell down in my room getting ready for school, he picked me up by my pants and set me back up on my feet. It was pretty cool. Shall I demonstrate?"

I could tell Ms. Blaine wanted to see it, but at the same time she wasn't sure whether it was appropriate. But the whole classroom started stomping and cheering, and it's not like I've ever gotten this much attention, well, this much positive attention.

"Sure. Go right ahead."

I looked over at Elvis. I was yammering on and on about him out of nervousness, and I never really checked in with him to see how he was feeling.

"Can we do this, boy?" I asked.

"You know I'm not a show pony, and this isn't show-and-tell," Elvis said.

I turned back to Ms. Blaine and told her I needed a moment to have a miniconference with my dog. Everyone laughed, but I didn't care. I walked toward the corner, and Elvis followed me.

"Please? Can you just help a guy out?"

"I appreciate you asking nicely, but I'm not really here for fun and games. I'm here to protect you."

"Really? What about our talk the other night about Taisy? You know, how you're just 'the temp' so we can relax the rules a little bit? Don't you think that should be a two-way street?"

Elvis looked at me very seriously. "You are smarter than you appear, and I will concede your point. You gave a fine argument, so I will acquiesce."

"I didn't understand anything you just said."

"I said fine, you're right, and let's get this over with."

I turned back around. "Okay, we're all set now. He gets stage fright sometimes and needs a pep talk." The class broke out in laughter again, and I could tell Ms. Blaine was also trying hard not to laugh.

I lay facedown on the floor, and soon all the kids were standing up so they could get a better view. Elvis, without missing a beat, simply leaned forward, grabbed me by my belt, and tossed his head up, and boom, I was standing upright again.

The applause was thunderous. Seriously, I've never heard anything like it. They asked me to do it again. So again, I lay down on the floor, and again he whipped me back up so I was on my feet. The room was cheering, and I have no problem admitting that it felt amazing. No wonder the twins loved being sports champions. It was pretty awesome to have my classmates yelling out my name. I couldn't help myself, I hugged Elvis. "Good boy. Thanks, buddy," I whispered into his fur.

"Let's do an encore, shall we?" he said back. "Tell them now I'll demonstrate what I'd do if someone came in to kidnap you."

"What?"

Ms. Blaine thought I was talking to her, so she responded, "Did you need something, Benji?"

"Uh, do you want to see one more thing?"

The classroom responded with more stomping and clapping. Ms. Blaine laughed and motioned for me to go on.

"Uh, this is what Elvis would do if someone came in to kidnap me."

"Well, this I have to see. Though I'm pretty sure that's not going to happen." Ms. Blaine laughed.

"Let's hope you're right." I went back and sat at my desk, but I was pretty nervous, because I had no idea what was about to happen next.

"Are you sure about this?"

Again, Ms. Blaine assumed I was talking to her because honestly, who else would she think I was talking to? Certainly not my talking dog! "It's only if you want to. If you're not comfortable, then we don't have to." This was met with boos from everyone in class.

I'm not sure who started it, but suddenly the kids were chanting, "Benji, Benji, Benji."

I guess I got swept up in the moment and just decided, what's the worst thing that could happen? I'd end up in the hospital again? So I nodded to Elvis that I was ready to go. Elvis barked three times and then ran over to the windows that lined the entire side of the wall. They were all open a few inches. He went from window to window, sticking his nose through the crack and opening up the window with the top of his head. Then he jumped up and looked out of each window, one by one. Next he ran over to my desk and pushed me out of my chair until I stood up. He grabbed me by the back of my pants like I was a bag of groceries and ran over to the third window, and with a toss of his head, he literally threw me out the window. It wasn't a far drop, just a foot or two, because I landed in some shrubs. Two seconds later Elvis jumped out the window himself, easily clearing the bushes. He walked back over to where I was still sprawled in the bushes, pulled me out, shook his head from side to side, which I guess was his way of shaking off all the leaves from me, and then set me upright on my feet.

When I looked up at the windows, all the kids were standing there cheering. Ms. Blaine looked totally freaked out over what had just happened, but she had a weird smile on her face too.

"Benji, are you okay?"

"I'm fine, Ms. Blaine. Thanks for asking." I said this even though I didn't mean it. I, too, was completely freaked out over what had just happened. I mean, my dog just threw me out of the window of my school classroom.

"That was the craziest thing I've ever seen. Elvis actually picked which window to toss you out of. I guess he knew the shrubs would break your fall."

"Yeah, I guess so. He's either really smart or he really doesn't like me." Everyone laughed at this, and I chuckled along to show everyone I found it amusing too.

"Well, come on back inside. But this time, I want both of you to use the door."

I nodded and headed to the front of the school. Elvis followed me, and as soon as we were alone, I turned to him.

"Are you crazy?! You threw me out a window! What kind of dog throws a person out the window? What if there weren't bushes below to break my fall?"

"Then I wouldn't have tossed you out. I would have found another way to save you. And it was better

145

than you being kidnapped."

"I wasn't being kidnapped, though! Why didn't you tell me what you were going to do?"

"Because if I had told you, you wouldn't have wanted to do it, and also, you would have gotten all tense, and that's when people really hurt themselves, because they're trying to break their fall. Trust me, it went much better because it was a surprise."

I didn't say anything else, mainly because it did seem like he knew what he was talking about, and also because I was still in shock from being thrown out of a window. When we walked back into the classroom, Elvis and I got a standing ovation. Elvis stood really tall and was pretty impressed with himself. When I took my seat, my heartbeat was still pounding in my head from the rush of it all, and I could feel that everyone was looking at me in a whole new way. It was a pretty good feeling.

Fifteen minutes later, my heart stopped beating so fast and the classroom was quiet as we worked on a long-division-problems sheet. I felt a tap on my back. I turned slightly, and Theresa Jenson passed me a note. Ms. Blaine was on the other side of the classroom, helping Kyle Duncan. (He is actually pretty good at math, but he always pretends he can't understand so Ms.

Blaine helps him.) Anyway, I took the note and glanced at it so I'd know who to pass it to, but the surprising thing was that it said my name on the front of it. I know this may be hard for you to understand, but this was the first note I had ever received in school. Who could it be from? What would it say? What if it wasn't a nice note? Was the person who wrote it staring at me right now?

My name was written in pink ink in flowery hand-writing. Whoever sent it had even dotted the *I* in my name with a flower that had a smiley face in the center. She'd colored in only every other petal of the flower, which made me think of that game I've seen girls play where they pluck the petals off flowers and say things like, "He loves me, he loves me not . . ." Could my note be a love note?

I was so nervous, I started to sweat. Suddenly Elvis's big face was in my face, and he whined, which I guess was his way of whispering.

"What are you doing? Are you feeling okay? You're breathing all funny. Please tell me you're not still think-ing about the window thing."

"I'm okay." I showed him the note that I'd just got.

"What's that?"

"It's a note."

"You shouldn't pass notes in class."

"I know that, but so what?"

"Benji?" I looked up and saw that Ms. Blaine was staring at me. "Is everything okay? Does Elvis need to go out?"

"Huh?"

"He's whining. Does that mean he needs to go outside?"

"I don't know. I only got him a few days ago, though it seems like longer."

"Well, if you've finished your assignment, you can take a hall pass and go outside for a moment, but you have to come right back."

"Yes, Ms. Blaine. Thank you."

My hand was on the door handle when she spoke again. "Aren't you forgetting something, Benji?"

"Please, excuse me, and thank you?"

The class cracked up, and I heard someone say, "Doofus." Oh well, my popularity was short-lived, but I didn't really care at that point.

"You forgot to take the hall pass." Ms. Blaine pointed to the wooden owl sitting on the bookshelf near her desk. That was the hall pass. I guess she figured if it was silly, then we wouldn't make up excuses just to get away, because we wouldn't want to be seen with this wooden owl in the hallways. Ms. Blaine was no dummy.

Before I could make a move, Elvis trotted over and carefully took the wooden owl by the red velvet ribbon on its neck and walked back over to meet me at the door. The whole classroom murmured. The dog had understood what she said. There was a burst of spontaneous applause.

Here's what I have to say about that. Elvis, I had now realized, was a big show-off. When we were walking down the hallway toward the front door, I told him as much.

"Well, I'd rather show off the skills that I currently have than break into a cold sweat when I receive a letter from a fellow classmate."

"Huh?"

"The note. Why are you so nervous about getting a note? Though for the record, I still disapprove of receiving silly notes from girls in class during school time. You're supposed to be working on your long division."

"How did you know it was from a girl?" I asked.

"Pink glittery ink? Plus it smells like strawberries. Oh yes, and I'm extremely smart—that's how I know." I'd smelled the note, but I couldn't smell anything.

"Well, now it just smells like your sweat and fear. But it did smell like strawberries before. Oh, is this the first note you've ever received from a girl?"

Elvis could really be a detective. He didn't miss a thing.

"Well, I'm going to go pay a visit to that Japanese maple tree over there while you read your note. I understand and respect the need for privacy. But please, Benjamin, pull it together. And for Pete's sake, stand up straight. Your posture is abhorrent. Your hands are shaking. It's a note from a girl, not a ransom note. Though even if it were a ransom note, we now know I'd be able to save you."

I turned away so he couldn't see me. Just when I was starting to like him again, he had to go say something like that to make me feel stupid. The note was written on regular notebook paper, the narrow-ruled kind, which I myself preferred over the fat-lined kind. The fat-lined paper gives you too much room for bad penmanship—at least that's what my mom always said. And this was certainly the case when it came to Taisy's awesomely girly handwriting.

This is what it said:

Dear Benji,
    I told my dog, Princess Daisy, all
about Elvis last night after I met him
in the hospital. She would like to invite

him over sometime. Princess Daisy is
a small dog, but she has a lot of friends
who are big dogs.

Cya later!! Taisy.

Taisy? Taisy? Taisy McDonald sent me a note? I couldn't believe it. If someone was going to push me off a cliff if I got the answer wrong, and they made me guess who this note was from, in a million billion years, I never would have thought it'd be her. I would have been pushed off that cliff and be flat as a pancake right now. I mean, sure she seemed totally into Elvis when she met him, but it was just so surprising she wrote notes in class. I didn't really think of her being a girlie girl.

At the end of the morgue tour, Dino had said again he had no idea that Taisy and I were around the same age. He said he would have introduced me a long time ago. He also said he was pretty sure he must have mentioned me to her anyway, because I was his favorite patient. I was really happy when he told me that. I suspected I was his favorite, despite my crazy mom, but it was nice to hear. He told me I should be friends with Taisy, because she was a special girl. I explained it was highly unlikely that Taisy and I would be friends, because she ran in a completely different social circle at school. What I didn't explain about our social circles was that she was popular and had lots of friends, and I didn't.

But now that I'd gotten this note, maybe I was wrong about all that. She did invite me over. Well, she invited my dog, but she had to know that I would have to come over too, right? Unless she thought that maybe I would just drop him off? What I couldn't get over was the whole pink pen girlie handwriting, since she was such a tomboy. She shoots free throws at recess. Let me tell you something, I doubt very seriously I could even make a free-throw basket. Well, perhaps I could, but I'd have to have good aim and do it granny-style, underhanded. I just don't have the arm strength to play basketball well. Or the coordination. Or the running skills. Or the aim.

A big drop of drool landed on my note, and I knew Elvis was back.

"Oh, so it was Taisy who wrote you the note? Did she say anything about me?" he asked. "What's Taisy short for, anyway? Why doesn't anyone want to go with their formal name anymore?"

"I don't know what it's short for, and who cares! She wrote me a note. Well, unless this isn't really from her and someone is just messing with me."

"What do you mean, messing with you?"

"I mean, maybe someone forged this note and signed her name to play a mean joke on me."

"You watch too much television. Why would someone do that?"

"I may watch a lot of television, but you have no idea what elementary school is like. Kids play mean jokes all the time."

"No, it's from her. I can tell." Elvis leaned in and smelled the note.

"Are you telling me you can smell that she wrote the note?"

"I can. And I can tell you that either her pen has strawberry-smelling ink or she was wearing strawberry lip gloss when she wrote it. But enough about her—have you met Princess Daisy?"

"Who?"

"Princess Daisy. Her dog. Is she a real princess?"

"Is who a real princess?"

"Princess Daisy. Is that a proper title? Is she of royal lineage?"

"Are you asking me if Taisy's dog is actual royalty, as in Prince William and Kate?" Yes, I know all about William and Kate, mainly because my mom woke me up early so I could watch their wedding on television with her. "I doubt it, Elvis."

"How disappointing. We would have made a suitable pair, given the fact that I'm to be the president's dog. And I find it rather silly to name someone Princess when she isn't actually a princess. What serious-minded canine would want to have such a name?"

"I'm pretty sure you're the last dog on earth who should be making fun of another dog's name, Mr. Parker Elvis Pembroke the Fourteenth."

"It's the Fourth, and you know it."

"Whatever! Who cares about all this? How would I know anything about Taisy's dog? I'm not friends with her. She's only spoken to me two times, ever! Well, maybe that's not true. Once when we were doing math races at the board, I beat her and she said, 'Good game, Barnsworth.' Athletes tend to call people by their last names. I guess it's because that's what's usually on the back of everyone's shirt."

"Well, I find Taisy to be a very upstanding young lady, despite her dog's silly name. And more important, I feel she would make a lovely choice for your pack."

"My pack? My pack of what?"

"Dogs are pack animals. Meaning we don't like to be alone, so we have a group of dogs that we hang out with, and we all look out for one another."

"I already have a family."

"I know, but your pack doesn't have to just be your family. It can be other dogs too. Usually they're more your peers, as opposed to your parents. Your parents have to like you. Your pack, you try to win their approval and respect. And from what I can tell, you need your own pack at school."

"Well, if we're supposed to be alike, then Taisy can't be in my pack. She could not be more different from me."

"If you don't know her, then how do you know she's so different?"

"Have you met me? I'm small, terrible at all sports, and sickly. She's like the total opposite of me. Even more so than the twins, because she's a girl."

"Benjamin, that's all outside stuff. You both have overbearing parents. Her dad seems a lot like your mom."

"You mean kinda scary intimidating?"

"Exactly. Speaking of, does your mother always sit outside your school in her car and wait for you all day?"

"What are you talking about?"

Elvis moved his head toward the street, and I saw what looked like my mom's car parked on the street. I walked over to get a closer look, because my mom has a bunch of stickers of the twins' all-star teams on her back window and . . . there they were. It was my mom's car.

"You know, if I may speak my mind . . ."

"Oh, now you're going to ask me?"

"Very funny, Benjamin. What I was about to say before I was so rudely interrupted was your mom seems very involved in your life."

"She is, but that's because I'm sick a lot."

"Yes, I figured that was why she showed up at the hospital that night to check on you while you were sleeping."

"What are you talking about? She did not."

"She did too. It was around midnight, and you were asleep. She came in and pulled the covers up over you and kissed you on your forehead. It was a very sweet moment and made me miss my own mother back in Tennessee."

"How do you know?"

"Because I was there, and I'm a very light sleeper. Even when I'm asleep I can hear stuff that's going on. It's a dog thing—you wouldn't understand, and I don't have the time or the patience to explain it to you. Now we should stop with all this dillydallying and head back to class. I want to stay on Ms. Blaine's good side. I liked her from the moment I smelled her."

"I want to go see why my mom is there."

"Maybe you shouldn't. From here it's hard to tell if she's even in the car. Maybe she just parked it there."

"Oh, and you can't tell with all your heightened dog senses? I would think you could smell whether she's in there or not."

Elvis didn't respond, which meant he knew she was in there and was just trying to get me back to class. I walked over to the car and knocked on the window. My mom was watching a movie on her phone, and I startled her. She screamed and threw her phone up in the air. She has good reflexes, so she caught it. She rolled down the window.

"Benji, for goodness' sake, get out of the street! Go around to the other side right this second."

I ran around to the passenger side, opened the door, and climbed in. I told Elvis to wait outside. This was a conversation between mother and son, not mother, son, and nosy dog.

"Mom, what are you doing?"

"I was watching a movie."

"I saw that. But why are you parked outside the school, watching a movie?"

"Benji, shouldn't you be in class?"

"I finished my work, and Ms. Blaine said I could take Elvis outside."

"Well, shouldn't you be getting back? I don't want her to worry."

"Mom, answer the question."

"Sometimes I sit outside the school."

"Why?"

"Benji, you'll understand this when you're older and have kids of your own. But sometimes you just need to be close to the ones you're worried about."

"Did you come back to the hospital after book club?"

"What?"

"Did you come back and check on me after book club and not tell me?"

"How do you know that?"

"It doesn't matter how I know, I just want to know if it's true."

"Benji, you're my baby and—"

"Mom, I'm not your—"

"Don't interrupt me. You are my baby, because you're my last child. And even though you're not allowed to ever talk about this again, I want to tell you something. You were really sick a lot when you were young. Really sick, and honestly, it scared me, because I don't know what I would have done if you didn't get better. So you were sick in the NICU and they wouldn't let me stay in there all night, and sometimes, when I couldn't sleep at night because I wasn't with you, I'd drive to the hospital and just sit outside in the parking lot, so that if you needed me, I'd be close by. It's a mother's job to be close by in case her kids need her. So here I am."

I didn't really know what to say to that. I had never heard my mother talk to me about myself like that before. She almost seemed like she was going to cry. I was more than a little freaked out.

"I should go back to class now."

"Okay."

"I love you, Mom."

"I love you too, Benji ba— I love you too, Benji."

"And don't forget I'm going to be eleven in seven months, which is only two years away from being a teenager."

"I know."

"And thanks for letting me get a dog."

"You're welcome."

# 9

Getting an awesome note in class has its pros and cons. The pros are it makes you feel special, it's cool to have a secret, and it gives you something to think about besides whatever is being taught in class. The con is that it puts you under a great deal of stress to write back a note as good as you received. As this was the very first note that I'd ever received in class, I didn't have experience on how to write a response, and since this response was going to be the very first note that I ever wrote in class in my whole entire life, I felt like it had to be perfect, because I was going to remember it for the rest of my life. Or I'd remember it at least for a while.

So during the rest of math I couldn't concentrate.

I kept thinking of what would make the coolest opening to my note. *Dear Taisy?* Nah, too boring. *Dearest Taisy?* No way, too girlie, and it sounded like those black-and-white movies my mom sometimes watches. *Yo, Taisy?* That sounded cooler, but it didn't sound like me at all. *Yo-Yo, Taisy?* No, that sounded like I was calling her a yo-yo, and what if she asked if I could yo-yo, and then I'd have to admit that I was not a good yo-yo-er at all? I suppose I could also try just Taisy, T, T-dawg, T-bird, or T.M. (Elvis suggested T-bone, but that's because he's a dog and was just thinking about steak. Note to self: Never ask a dog's opinion when he's hungry.) *Hey, Tais?* Oh, that sounded good. Casual, yet cool. Friendly, but not overeager.

After much agonizing, that's exactly what I ended up with, *Dear Taisy.* Now I had two words, a blank piece of paper, and a sweaty pencil. Eventually I decided to stop worrying so much, be myself, and hope for the best. Short and sweet. I mean, it's not like she was expecting Shakespeare. At least I hope she wasn't.

This is what I wrote:

Dear Taisy,
    How are you? I am fine. Thank you for
your note. Yes, Elvis and I would find it cool

to meet Princess Daisy. I'm sure Princess Daisy is cuter than Elvis, because she's smaller and drools a lot less. Elvis doesn't have any dog friends yet, so it would be nice for them to meet. Okay, I should get back to math now, because these problems aren't going to solve themselves. Ha, ha.

Sincerely, Benji (and Elvis)

My mom once bought me an origami kit during one of my hospital stays, so I know how to make a crane, a camera, a balloon that you can actually blow up, and a frog. I decided to use my skills on Taisy's note. I wished I knew how to fold the note into a flower, but that one was kinda complicated. I decided to fold it into a little frog, and when I finished, you could press the butt down with your finger and it would hop a little like a frog. After I was done folding it up, I wrote her name on its back. Now I just had to figure out how I was going to get it to her.

I whispered to Elvis to see if he had any ideas. Elvis said that he was not going to be an accomplice to bad behavior.

"Fine, if you don't want to have tea with Princess Daisy, then that's okay with me. I bet there'll be scones."

I don't even know what a scone is, but I've heard my mom talk about them, and she says they're delicious. I figured since Elvis was Mr. Fancy-Pants, he probably knew all about tea and scones.

"Fine, but we'll do it before lunch. And speaking of, I hear if you actually pay attention in school, you might learn more." I stuck my tongue out at him in response. What he didn't know was that before today, all I ever did in school was learn.

Right before lunch Elvis shoved his face in my face and licked me.

"Put the note in my mouth."

"No, you'll get it all gross and wet."

He licked his tongue dry on my pants. "Now do it. This is the driest my tongue gets."

I placed the frog on his tongue and watched as he trotted over to the back of the class. He stopped behind Taisy's chair. She turned to pet him, and he must have opened his mouth and stuck out his tongue, because I saw her look around quickly and grab the note. She then fawned all over Elvis, pressing her face into his black velvety cheek while also rubbing his furry nose at the same time. He clearly loved it. He wagged his tail so hard he whacked the globe right off the table behind him. Before anyone could react, the bell rang and everyone made a break for the door.

It didn't look like Taisy was ever going to stop petting Elvis. He was now lying on the floor on his back, and it was clear he wasn't going anywhere anytime soon either. I guess he felt like he deserved a big, long belly rub from a cute girl after his kidnapping save. I had no choice but to go over there.

"Uh, hey, Taisy."

"Who's-d'-loving-belly-wub?Who's-d'-biggest-belly-in-da-whole-wide-world? Who's-d'-best-puppy-ever? You are, yes you are." Taisy didn't even hear me.

It really was a hilarious sight to see her baby-talking like that, because you should see her on the basketball court. She's fierce, and even gives our PE teacher, Coach Connor, a run for his money when they play one-on-one basketball. I've never seen someone so competitive during PE. She wins every race, every basketball contest. When we did square dancing, she even found a way to be the best at that too.

"Hey, Taisy," I said again.

Finally she turned and saw me, and I guess she realized she sounded pretty silly, because she gave me a shy smile. "Hey, Benj."

I couldn't help it. I loved when she called me Benj! She said it like she'd known me her whole life and we had been best buddies forever, not just new acquain-tances.

"So I see you really like dogs," I said.

"I don't like dogs. I love dogs. And I've never met a dog so big before. He's like me. Big, strong, and super-cute."

Ms. Blaine walked over and joined the party. "Hey, guys, I hate to break this up, but you should head for lunch now. I've got to go get some coffee in the teach-ers' lounge."

We nodded and walked to the door together. I swear Elvis was a little drunk from his belly rub. He was sorta woozy, and his tail was the highest I'd ever seen. When we got out into the hallway, Taisy threw her arms around Elvis again, giving him a big kiss on the cheek. Then she headed off to the cafeteria.

"Aren't you coming?" she asked, turning around.

Elvis walked toward her, but then stopped when he realized I had fallen silent. Behind Taisy, another ten feet up the hallway, I saw Billy Thompson. He was yelling at a kid I didn't recognize in the hallway. I auto-matically reached into my pocket for my lug nut, but of course it wasn't there. I swallowed uneasily.

"Uh, you go on ahead, Taisy. I gotta hit the little boys' room." Oh great, now I'd just sounded like a six-year-old, but I couldn't worry about that now. I was too worried about making a run for it before Billy Thompson saw me.

Taisy nodded. "Bye, Elvis! Later, Benj!"

Elvis and I watched her go. I silently pleaded for her to hurry up and round the corner so I could take off in the other direction before Billy Thompson spotted me.

"It was her lip gloss," said Elvis.

"What was?" I whispered.

"It was her lip gloss that smelled like strawberries. She's my new favorite person, after the president, of course, and my own mom. Her belly rubs are just extraordinary, and I think you should . . ."

Before he finished his sentence, I turned and speed-walked in the opposite direction. Then I felt someone grab the back of my shirt. I took a deep breath and exhaled loudly.

"Elvis, I really hope that's you."

"Of course it is—who else would it be? Ralph Waldo Emerson?"

"Who?"

"Ralph Waldo Emerson, the poet? Oh, never mind. It's not important. Now, you're heading in the wrong direction for the lunchroom. C'mon, let's get some food. I'm starving. Belly rubs make me extra hungry." Elvis lifted his nose in the air and took a whiff. "Chicken-fried steak and hot dogs, I think." He started to walk back down the hall in the opposite direction. After a moment, he stopped and looked at me, because I hadn't moved.

"Uh, I don't usually eat lunch in the cafeteria."

"What do you mean?"

"Well, I bring my lunch and eat in the library, with the librarian, Ms. Hensel."

"You're not supposed to bring food into a library."

"How do you know? You've never been in a library before."

"I have too. During my extensive training, I was taken into a library in Nashville, and I saw lots of signs that said no food or drink. No one wants to borrow a book that is all sticky with food. C'mon, Benjamin, there are about ten chicken-fried steak patties with my name on them."

"Relax, I brought you food too."

"Is it warm and round and shaped like chicken-fried steak?"

"No. It's kibble and a bag of Doritos."

"If it's all the same to you, I would much prefer to have chicken-fried steak."

I stood there for a second longer, not knowing what to do. Well, there was no point to having any secrets, I thought, because it wasn't like he wouldn't eventually figure it out on his own.

"I don't eat in the cafeteria because I don't have anyone to sit with," I confessed.

"You can sit anywhere in a cafeteria," Elvis said. "That's the whole point of a democracy. You know, the whole it's-a-free-country thing. Don't tell me I'm going to have to start teaching you about American history."

"I mean no one wants to sit with me. I don't have a pack here at school." I decided to put it in dog language.

"Well, now you have me, so let's go eat together. C'mon, I'm certain the chicken-fried steak is going to run out before the hot dogs."

"I don't know—Ms. Hensel, the librarian, might worry if I don't show up."

"Benjamin, please stop this. You're a kid. You're in school, you're supposed to eat in the cafeteria with other kids. How are you going to create a pack if you hide and don't talk to anyone? You barely even spoke to Taisy, and she showed every sign of being quite friendly to you, and now that she clearly adores me, I'm sure that will only make your case stronger. Why can't you sit with her at lunch?"

"Are you kidding me? Taisy is the best athlete in this town. She may even break the twins' record for number of trophies earned in one year. She has a super-famous dad. She sits anywhere she wants. People usually beg her to sit with them at lunch. Plus she usually eats fast and then goes outside and practices basketball."

"Benjamin. I'm not going to eat in the library. Maybe you can eat neatly enough to be allowed to do so, but I cannot. I'm a dog, I eat off the floor, and when I think about food, I produce a large quantity of saliva. It's a physiological response that is Pavlovian and is a long story that I can't get into right now, especially when I'm hungry. When I eat, we will need to have a large number of napkins."

And with that he came up behind me and nudged me so I moved forward.

"Hey, don't push me," I said.

"Please, that was the tiniest of nudges. Move. Now." I hesitated, and Elvis asked me, "Is there something else that's the matter?"

"Well, I saw Billy Thompson over there, and usually when I see him, I walk in the other direction. It's called survival of the fittest."

"Actually, that's not the right usage of that terminology. Survival of the fittest means—"

"Elvis, I know what it means. I was making a joke. Forget it."

"Look, I know this Billy chap was giving you difficulties before, but things are different now. He may be tough, but trust me, I'm tough too. Especially when I'm hungry. Now, start walking."

"Fine. But who died and made you king of the world?"

"Didn't you hear Taisy? I'm the best fuzziest face in da whole wide world."

# 10

I hadn't eaten in the cafeteria since the first week of school this year, so I forgot how loud it could get. After I waited in line for a hot lunch and used my emergency sneaker money (my mom always makes me put a twenty-dollar bill in my sneaker) to buy chicken-fried steak—five for Elvis, one for me—lunch was already half over, and some of the tables were empty. So I took my tray and sat down at an empty table over by the far wall.

"Well, no wonder you don't have anyone in your pack. You don't even try to be social. Why not go sit at one of the tables with kids?"

I explained to Elvis that he might know a lot of stuff, but he didn't know anything about the school cafeteria. He didn't know that for someone like me, it's filled with rejection. I actually started school one week after everyone else, because I had an ear infection that gave me vertigo so I couldn't get out of bed without falling down. By the time I got there, I didn't know how lunchtime worked in the fourth grade. Basically, you can't sit at a table unless you're invited. I made that mistake on my first day, and it wasn't pretty. No one let me sit at their table, mainly because where you sit in the lunchroom is all about status, and I had none. It's like a nice neighborhood where you don't want to get that one neighbor who puts up some puny little house smack in the middle of all these super-nice mansions. I just didn't fit in. Third grade wasn't like this, but in fourth grade you were considered an "upperclassman" with the fifth graders. And then in sixth grade you moved to the junior high building and had to start all over at the bottom of the heap.

I don't know why I even bothered explaining it to Elvis, because he wasn't paying attention to anything

I said. He just watched me cut up his chicken-fried steak patties and drooled. He wasn't kidding about those napkins. I mixed the chicken-fried steak with his kibble and then started to eat my own food. A minute later, a group of boys stood right next to me while I ate.

"This is our table," said Travis, their leader.

"Oh, I'm sorry."

"Did we say you could sit here at our table?"

"No, you didn't. I'll move." I stood up and picked up my tray.

"I didn't tell you to move." Travis took a step toward me. His hair was so long, it covered his eyes. I wondered how he could see. I sat back down.

"We don't need the table now because we're going out to play kickball. But we wanted to tell you that this is our table and you're not allowed to sit here again."

"Okay, I get it. It's your table."

Just as Travis was about to turn and leave, up walked Billy Thompson with his gang of thugs. This was the last thing I needed. I could have been eating my lunch peacefully in the library. Instead, the two meanest kids in the school were standing a foot away from me and having a face-off. Billy leaned down and put his face about an inch away from Travis's. Travis was a year older, but Billy was bigger. I sat back, ready to duck. I didn't want to be in the way if Billy started spitting.

"What's going on here, Travis?" Billy glared.

"None of your business, Billy." Travis tried to stand taller.

"I said what's going on here, Travis?" Billy repeated slowly, leaning in even closer. Travis shrank back.

"Nothing's going on, Billy. He's sitting at my table, and I was just letting him know that's not allowed."

"So this is your table? I don't see your name on it." Billy pretended to look all around the table.

Okay, now I was confused. Was Billy Thompson standing up for me? Was he defending my honor?

"Everyone knows it's my table, Billy, so cut it out. Don't tell me you care about this skinny sack of bones and his fat, dumb dog."

Skinny sack of bones? I had been called a lot of things in my life, but skinny sack of bones had never made the list. And I didn't even want to look at Elvis. There was no way he would take being called fat and dumb lightly. I was mad and scared, but I also found the whole scene kind of exciting. Billy and Travis fighting? This was the best bully matchup in the St. Elmo's Street Elementary School history.

"What's it to you what I care about?" asked Billy.

"Why are you so interested in me? Do you want me to come over and play hopscotch at your house after school? I bet you have that big bucket of colored chalk and you draw pictures of rainbows and hearts on your driveway."

Travis blushed. I knew he regretted ever coming over to the table. I hoped he wouldn't take his humiliation out on me in the future, when Billy wasn't around. The last thing I needed was a new bully on my roster.

"Shut up, Billy. We're out of here. I've got a kickball game to get to."

"Well, don't let me stop you."

Travis and his boys walked off, which left me with Billy Thompson and his own gang of thugs, who were now all grinning and high-fiving one another. I guess in the battle of the bullies, their leader had just won. I didn't know what to say. I found the whole thing pretty odd. Billy was being territorial over me, like I was his prize punching bag and Travis couldn't have me.

"What are you staring at?" he asked, glaring at me this time.

"M-m-me? Nothing. I, uh, nothing. Sorry?"

"You should be!"

He slammed his fist so hard on the table, my chicken-fried steak patty flew up an inch off my tray into the air. It caught me off guard, and I think I actually squeaked. Elvis moved into the space between Billy and me. They had a major bully versus dog stare-down contest. This time Billy didn't win. I wouldn't say Elvis won, either. It was more like a draw. Billy just walked away. I breathed a sigh of relief. I guess Elvis was right: Billy wasn't bright, but he wasn't dumb enough to go after me and a giant dog.

Of course, just when I thought I was safe, Billy turned around and left me with some parting words. "So did you hear about the new nerd in school? He's got brain issues just like you. Maybe you two can be weirdo BFFs," he said, laughing.

"Thanks, but I've already got enough friends."

"Really? Is that why you're sitting here eating lunch with your fat dog?"

"Look, pick on me all you want, but don't call my dog fat. He's not fat. He's big boned."

"Whatever, dude." He laughed again. "How come you're not hiding out in the library eating lunch with your girlfriend the librarian?"

For some reason this comment hit me hard. I was surprised Billy knew about the library. I had always assumed no one even thought about me, so they'd never notice if I ate in the library. The next thing I knew, the boys behind Billy slowly backed up, and I had no idea why. I guess I was so distracted by Billy glaring down at me, I didn't hear what was happening. Then I heard it, a low buzzing like a giant swarm of bees in this movie I once saw or the low-octave hum of a motorcycle gang riding down the highway in the distance. Then I realized it was coming from Elvis. He looked completely normal. His mouth was closed. But it was an unmistakable sound, the low growl of a dog. He stared at the boys intently.

"Anyway, Billy, my chicken-fried steak is getting cold, so unless there was something you wanted to talk to me about specifically, I'm just going to eat my lunch. Okay?"

"Okay, lamebrain Benji, you do that. Come on, guys, let's bail. It smells over here."

And just like that they walked off. The whole thing probably only lasted five minutes, but it felt like an eternity. I was so stressed, I actually forgot to faint. I turned to Elvis.

"Eating in the library doesn't look so bad anymore, does it? Hey, was that you growling?"

"No."

"It was too! That's cool how you can do that without opening your mouth."

There were only ten more minutes left until the bell rang. Then I had art class, then PE (which I got to sit out of because of my wrist), then back to Ms. Blaine's class and then the day was over. I looked over at Elvis. He had licked his plate clean. Literally.

"Hey do you want the rest of my—"

"—lunch?" he said, finishing my sentence.

Elvis cocked his head to the side, and I turned to see what he looking at.

I heard chanting, low and rhythmic. It took me a second to figure out what everyone was saying. "New kid! New kid! New kid!" they chanted. Coach Connor stood up from the teachers' table and blew his whistle, and the chanting stopped. That man doesn't go anywhere without wearing his whistle. Like, I bet he wears it in the shower and sleeps with it.

Then I saw him, the new kid everyone was talking about. He was standing by the cafeteria cashier, scanning the room for a safe place to sit. I recognized his expression immediately. It was terror. Just looking at his face made my stomach hurt, so I looked away.

"Hey, you should wave him over here," Elvis suggested.

"What? No way," I said.

"Benjamin, he's new. He doesn't know anyone. We

have room at our table."

"You mean the table no one is sitting at because I don't have any friends? So now you want me to risk falling even lower on the scale of nobodies in this place by inviting the new kid to sit with us? Didn't you see what just happened a minute ago? I had two of the meanest bullies in the entire school fighting over me. I'm already a target, and now you want me to basically shoot off a flare gun so we can have a second go-around? Forget it. I don't know about you, but I'd like to make it to art class today. There's a Popsicle-stick log cabin project I'm trying to finish."

"It's the right thing to do."

"Says who?"

"Says me. And you of all people should be empathetic to his plight. He's new, and alone. You can add him to your pack."

"Shut up about my pack. I'm not a dog. I'm a kid. If you want to add him to your pack, you go over and sit with him."

Elvis let out a short, sharp bark. Everyone turned to look at us, including the new kid. This was a disaster. A new emotion flashed over the kid's face. It was just a split second, but I caught it and recognized it immediately. It was hope. Now I really had no choice, so I waved him to come over to my table. He smiled and headed our way. I turned to Elvis.

"Happy? I'm basically a sitting duck now."

"What does that mean?"

"It means you have no right to boss me around like this. You're new, and you don't understand how elementary school works."

"It was the right thing to do," Elvis insisted.

"So what? Don't you get it? You're the dog and I'm the master. I'm supposed to tell you what to do, not the other way around."

"First off, I'm not your dog. And second, in this pack, I'm clearly the alpha, which means I'm in charge of you."

"Oh, here we go, how could I possibly forget? All you do is remind me. You're the president's dog. I get it. So go be the president's dog then! I'll wear my stupid helmet tomorrow if it means you'll stop meddling in my life. You do realize you're only making my life harder for me, right? And don't forget, you threw me out of a window!"

"I did it to save you!"

"You did it to show off! I thought you were here to help me, to protect me, but no, what you're doing is making me an even bigger target than I used to be."

"Benjamin, calm down. I didn't mean to make you so upset. I just wanted you to do the right thing and—"

Just then the new kid put his tray down on the table. He looked at me and then at Elvis, realizing we were in the middle of something serious.

"I forgot my milk. I'm going to go get it. May I get you or your dog something while I'm up there?" he asked.

"No, thanks." The new kid walked off, and we went back to our fight.

"I know it's the right thing to do. I'm not stupid. But it's easy for you to be all high and mighty about doing the right thing when you're big and strong and smarter than everyone else. But it's not so easy for the rest of us. You just don't understand what it's like to be me."

"Don't tell me I don't understand. I understand plenty. I'll have you know I was born the runt of my litter. And in the dog world, that means I was born a nobody. A lot of times the runt doesn't even survive. You know why? Sometimes the mother rejects the runt and doesn't feed it enough because she wants to save her milk for the other puppies, the stronger ones."

"Are you going to tell me you were kicked out of your litter and raised by wolves? Or a duck? Or better yet, you went out into the woods and built yourself a doghouse out of twigs and survived on berries?" I asked.

"Don't be a smart aleck. No, my mom didn't do that, but it could have happened. And I will tell you one thing. My littermates shunned me. They never let me hang out with them, because I was scrawny and small. When I went to get water, they flipped me into the water bowl. They called me Puny Pembroke. Or Tiny Whiney Woofy. But you know what I did? I'll tell you. I ate a lot, I slept a lot, and I studied a lot. I trained four times longer and harder than every other dog there. I asked a lot of questions. I observed the world around me. And though everyone said there was no way I would ever get picked to be anyone's dog, I never believed it. I knew I was special, and I knew I worked harder than every other dog. And two years ago, when word on the farm was that the president of the United States was coming to select a dog for himself, I was prepared. Lola Beth was so excited about him visiting that she read everything about him she could get her hands on. I knew his favorite color. I knew he had a good sense of humor. I knew he had a childhood dog that played dead when he pointed a finger gun at him and went bang-bang. So when he pointed that finger gun at me, like I hoped he would, I staggered around and flopped over and played dead better than any other dog in the history of the world. And he picked me. So don't tell me I don't know what it's like to be the underdog. I know plenty. Don't let anyone tell you who you are, Benjamin, especially when they don't even know you. Be who you want to be."

"Yeah, oh yeah? Well . . ." I didn't really have a response, because that was a pretty awesome story. But I was mad, really mad, and so I sort of lost my temper.

"You know what, I think you're lying. That's it. You're a liar. Liar, liar, furry butt on fire! I don't believe any of it. I don't believe you were the runt, and I don't believe you're the president's dog. I think you're making it all up so you can act superior to everyone you meet, and hog all the attention for yourself."

Oh boy, I knew I'd crossed the line right at the exact moment the words came out of my mouth, but I couldn't stop myself. Luckily, the new kid was back, standing next to me with two cartons of milk. He looked at me and then at Elvis, and then at me again.

"Did you just call your dog a liar?"

"I did."

"Here, you look like you could use some milk." He held out one of the red milk cartons toward me. I didn't know what else to do, so I took it. He sat down and calmly ate his lunch.

"My name is Benji," I said. "So I guess from all the

chanting you're the new kid?"

"Yes. I started school two weeks ago. I think my first day was the day you had your medical emergency in the hallway and went to the hospital. My name is Alexander Chang-Cohen, but I go by Alexander. I appreciate you inviting me to sit with you and your Newfie dog."

"You know the breed?"

"I have total recall, which means I remember every single thing I see, hear, experience, everything. I think I saw a picture of a Newfoundland in a book once. Lewis and Clark had a Newfie. He's very handsome, regal even."

"Well, don't get too used to him. He's not even my dog. He's a temp. I'm just waiting for my real dog."

"Oh."

This was when I noticed Alexander didn't have a backpack but instead had parked his rolling laptop bag next to our table. Oh, now it made sense.

"Hey, now I remember seeing you that day. Actually, it was one of the last things I remember seeing before my episode." I immediately pictured Alexander's rolling laptop bag in my mind. "Wasn't Billy Thompson giving you a hard time?"

"Yes, if by 'hard time' you mean he dumped all my

stuff on my head and then proceeded to kick it all over the hallway. I'm still finding things with his sneaker prints on them. It probably would have gotten worse, but you had your . . ." He trailed off, suddenly realizing maybe it was a sensitive issue for me.

"You mean my seizure? Well, at least it was good timing for you. So you saw the whole thing?"

"I did."

"And I guess you remember it pretty well, huh?"

"I remember it exactly. It was scary to see. Did you want to know something about—"

Alexander didn't get to finish his sentence, because a carton of milk sailed across the cafeteria and hit our table like a bomb, sending milk everywhere. I was stunned. Before I could react, another one came straight toward my head. Elvis leaped into the air, and it hit him instead of me. I couldn't believe he took a milk carton in the chest for me just like that. I guess he wasn't kidding when he said he'd take a bullet for the president. Next thing I knew, Elvis grabbed me by my shirt and pulled me under the table for cover. He was already going after Alexander when the third milk carton hit. There was total chaos in the lunchroom. Kids screamed, teachers shouted, and Elvis barked a totally different bark than I had ever heard before. This bark was deep and scary and very serious.

I wiped my face off on my T-shirt. I looked over at Alexander, sitting calmly under the table with me.

"You okay?" I asked.

"Me? Oh, sure. Do you regret asking me to sit with you now?"

"No," I said, but I didn't know if I meant it.

"I'm not sure if I would have done the same if our roles were reversed. I like to believe I would have, but I can be a big chicken sometimes. Anyway, you were really brave to put yourself out there for me, especially knowing there would be consequences if you did. I'm just happy it wasn't a milk carton full of ketchup and peas."

"Ooh, that's disgusting. Did that happen to you before?"

"Yup, it happened at my last school, but lucky for me the kid had bad aim, so it missed me and hit our vice principal in the back."

Alexander cracked up, and just the thought of a milk carton full of ketchup hitting Principal Kriesky made me crack up too. Pretty soon the two of us were hysterically laughing under the lunchroom table. Elvis finally stuck his head under to check on us.

"I gotta get you two out of here. How do you two feel about crawling through an air shaft?"

"Uh, I tend to get a little sweaty in small, confined spaces," I said to Elvis. Alexander thought I was talking to him. He looked worried.

"Me too! And there's always a rat up there, and I don't like their beady eyes."

"Me too!"

Wow, Alexander and I were so much alike. I couldn't believe how easy it was to hang out with him.

"So, we're just going to stand here and take this?" asked Elvis, who stuck his head under the table to talk to me.

"Elvis, it's okay. The bell's going to ring soon anyway. Sometimes it's not about fighting back, it's about waiting it out."

Right then Elvis got hit with a carton of chocolate milk, which splashed all over his back and dripped down his furry face. He barely flinched, though he was about to lick his nose when I yelled at him to stop. "Nooooooooooooo! That was chocolate milk! Don't taste it. Chocolate is bad for dogs!" I started to climb out from under the table.

Elvis was surprised, but he didn't say anything right away. He just wagged his tail a little bit, nudged me back under the table, and then proceeded to shake off all the excess milk.

After he finished shaking, he said, "Trust me, it'd take a lot more than chocolate milk to take me down."

"Hey, Alexander, can I ask you something?" I asked.

"Certainly."

"I have this thing, its kind of a lucky charm that my dad gave me, and well, the last time I had it was the day of my episode, and I'm wondering if maybe you happened to see it when you saw me go down. . . ."

"Was it a little shiny silver thing on a brown leather string?"

"Yes, it is. That's unbelievable! You remember it?"

"Benji, it's like my eyes are a video camera and I record everything I see, and so I can go back and see it all again if I think about it. I didn't know it was yours. I saw it on the floor, and for some reason I assumed it was Billy's."

"Billy's? Why would you think that? Wait a second, are you saying Billy has it?"

"Uh, no, I'm not saying that. I'm saying I saw it, and I thought it was his and then . . ."

Suddenly I was hopeful. Maybe it wasn't gone forever. Maybe I could get it back somehow. "I'm so relieved it's not gone. It's really important to me, and I thought it was lost forever. Do you think he still has it?"

"Uh, well . . . I don't know about that. I'm not saying I know for sure he has it or anything."

Just then I noticed a pair of pink Converse high-tops with yellow daisies next to me, and then a second later Taisy bent down and peered at us under the table.

"Hey, you guys okay?" she asked.

"Hey, Taisy. Yeah, we're fine. But guess what—Alexander's amazing brain has helped me find the good luck charm that I lost. Billy Thompson stole it."

"What? He did?"

"Wait, I never said Billy stole it," Alexander interjected.

Taisy interrupted, "Well it makes sense, because everyone knows Billy's a thief and a liar. Ooh, there's nothing I hate more than liars."

I nodded my head in agreement. "Yeah, me too. What about you, Alexander, don't you hate liars also?"

Alexander nodded, but he looked really stressed out, more stressed out now than when the milk bombs were flying. I wondered if he was shy around girls and Taisy was making him nervous.

"Hey, Taisy, this is my new friend, Alexander. He's

the new kid. And Alexander, this is Taisy, star athlete of our school."

"Well, first off, I don't think of myself as *the* star athlete of the school but as one of the star athletes of the school. And I want to be known for more than just that, so I'm also good at the flute, double Dutch jump rope, hair braiding, and super-swirly cursive writing. But I already know Alexander, because we have band together. He can play almost every single instrument. It's pretty out-of-control cool."

"Is the coast clear now?" I asked.

She disappeared for a second to look around the lunchroom and then popped down again. "Yep. All clear."

I believed her. There was no way anyone would throw anything with Taisy around. She'd just catch it and throw it right back, but with better aim. Alexander and I crawled out from under the table and looked around. The cafeteria was almost empty. Taisy grabbed some napkins and wiped Elvis down.

"Oh, my poor baby Elvis, did you get milky-wilky all over you?"

There she went with that baby talk again. Alexander looked surprised too. I just rolled my eyes and shrugged. Elvis had already forgotten all about

Alexander and me. He was basking in the glory of Taisy again.

"Hey, Benji, I need to talk to you about something," Alexander said, but before he could continue, Mr. D, the art teacher, walked over to us.

"Hey, you kids okay?" he asked.

We all nodded. We were actually all okay.

"Maybe everyone should go down to the principal's office and talk about what happened here."

Oh brother, that's the last thing we thought we should do. Alexander looked down at the ground. Taisy wasn't sure what to say, mainly because she wasn't really involved. Just the mention of the principal's office made her bottom lip quiver. It was up to me to say something.

"Mr. D, I think since nobody was injured, we should just let it go. We're okay, and it's not like we even know what happened. I mean, we do, but it's not like any of us saw who threw those milk cartons at us. Do we have to bother Principal Kriesky with this?"

I could tell he wasn't sure what to do. Mr. D was the most liberal teacher in school, being an artist and all. Word around the hallways was that he went to some fancy art school in New York, maybe had a nervous breakdown, and now has his own studio in some barn out in the countryside. So Mr. D wasn't a guy who played by the rules. He had cool tattoos and pierced ears. He sometimes even brought in his Bluetooth speakers and played music during art class, which I'm pretty sure is forbidden in our school.

"Yeah, Mr. D, we're good now," Taisy said. "And you know how Principal Kriesky gets after lunch."

On more than one occasion, we'd heard rumors that Principal Kriesky had a fussy stomach. If you were unlucky enough to see him when his stomach hurt, it never worked out in your favor.

"Also, it's a biological fact that people get sleepier after lunch, as their body is working hard at digesting their food properly. Why put more on his plate, especially since he's already just cleaned one," Alexander said, chuckling nervously at his own bad joke. "Get it? He just cleaned his plate, and now—"

"We get it, Alexander. Thanks," I said. "Mr. D, do you really want to be the guy who brings Principal Kriesky more bad news?"

"You know what they say, the messenger always gets killed," Taisy added.

Mr. D didn't need further convincing. I guess you never grow out of not wanting to go to the principal's office. So he said he'd walk us to our next class. Elvis and I were already going to art class with Mr. D; Taisy and Alexander had band. Alexander thought it would be best if we all met up after school to debrief. I'm not sure what that meant exactly, but it sounded cool so I agreed. Taisy said she was game to huddle up then too. We agreed to meet on the front steps after the last bell.

We headed down the hallway together, but Taisy and Alexander headed left to the band room while Mr. D, Elvis, and I went to the right. Art is in the next building over, because we are sharing the art room with the junior high kids for a month while some of our classrooms are getting new windows. Mr. D asked if Elvis and I were okay, and I said we were but I needed to give Elvis a quick run outside. Mr. D. nodded and then held out his fist to me. I guess he wanted me to fist-bump him, and even though I felt silly doing it, I knocked my fist into his.

"Thanks, Mr. D. I'll be back in class in a sec."

And that was that. Elvis and I walked outside. He sniffed around and peed on a few plants, but neither of us said anything. Clearly neither of us wanted to be the one to speak first. My mom says I can be stubborn when I want, but obviously so could Elvis. After everything that had just happened in the cafeteria, neither one of us wanted to admit we were sorry about our fight.

We slipped into art class only a few minutes late. As soon as I took my seat and started working on my log cabin, Elvis fell asleep. I wasn't sure how he'd be able to sense if anything was about to happen in my brain when he was snoring and drooling all over the classroom floor, but I didn't care.

I worked on the roof of my cabin, gluing Popsicle sticks together. I thought about lunch, and what Alexander Chang-Cohen had said about me being brave. No one in the history of my entire life had ever called me brave. Okay, that's not true. They had. People said it to me all the time in the hospital, but they only said it because everyone thinks hospitals are such scary places. They assumed I was scared there, and therefore I was brave. But that wasn't really the case. I'm comfortable at the hospital. Everyone knows me, I know everyone, and it's a world that's far more familiar to me than school. Let's put it this way: no one throws milk cartons at you while you're in the hospital. And I'm in the hospital because I have no choice.

But I did have the choice to ask Alexander to sit with us at lunch. Even if it was technically Elvis's idea to do it, it was my action that made everything happen. I had never really put myself out there like that before. In fact, usually it was people who put themselves out there for me. It felt good that I could finally pay it forward. I also thought about my titanium lug nut. If Billy had it, like Alexander said, I would never get it back from him. It was a little weird how Alexander's brain was like a video recorder, and I realized I could finally figure out what had happened to me that day. It was scary not knowing what was wrong with me, but I wondered whether the truth was even scarier.

But right now, above all else, my biggest problem was Elvis. I knew he was still mad at me about our fight. I was still angry about it too. But I really regretted calling him a liar. Sometimes when I get mad, I lose control and say things I don't mean. My emotions go into overdrive, and I can't control my mouth anymore. I knew I sounded like a baby saying he'd started the fight, but it was true. He totally started it. Why was Elvis so pushy about me asking Alexander to sit with us at lunch? If I hadn't waved him over for lunch, all that milk carton bombing would never have happened. But then again, when I thought about it, I was happy I'd met Alexander. He seemed pretty cool. I wondered what it was he needed to talk to me about before Mr. D interrupted. Seeing that I had never really made a friend like him so quickly, I wondered whether it was something you discussed, like "Hey, do you want to be friends, or what?" Or whether it just sort of happened on its own.

Maybe Elvis had a point about this whole pack thing. It's not like I hadn't noticed that I didn't have many friends. My life is just so busy between the hospital, my mom, trying to avoid getting noogies by the twins, and looking at sock catalogs for new and interesting socks, I never noticed before. I've always thought of myself as more of a loner. Maybe that was changing, I thought. And of course, it was way more fun sitting under the table with Alexander than being by myself. And it was so nice of Taisy to come over and check on us afterward. Maybe she would be part of my pack too? I even had to admit, when I really thought about it, that it had been nice talking to Elvis. He could be really great company. Then again, like he said, he's not even my real dog.

# 11

I was more than ready to go home once the school day was finally over. When it's cold or raining I usually take the school bus, but I don't live that far from school, and mostly I like to walk. After

school my mom is busy taking the twins to one of their many sports practices, and I like to get all my homework done right away. The bus isn't that bad, mainly because I sit up front by the bus driver, but that has its own perils. Our bus driver is a million years old, and he wears glasses that are as thick as Coke bottles. I'm not sure he's the best guy to drive a bunch of kids to and from school.

Anyway, I told Elvis that we were going to walk home, and then he reminded me we had promised to meet Alexander and Taisy after school. These were the first words he had spoken to me since our big fight at lunch.

"That's right," I said. "Thanks for reminding me. I can't believe I forgot. It's been a long day."

"For you and and me both," he said coldly.

Clearly he was still upset with me. I guessed dogs held grudges. We walked around to the front of the school to look for Alexander, but when we got out to the steps, they were almost empty. I didn't see Alexander anywhere.

"Maybe he forgot," I said.

"Somehow I doubt that."

"Oh right, I guess a kid with total recall doesn't forget anything! Let's wait then."

During art class, Mr. D had explained more to me about Alexander and his total recall brain. He told me Alexander can look at a painting and then do a perfect reproduction of it with crayons. He said it was super-cool to watch.

"I'm thirsty. Do you think you can hold the water fountain button for me?" asked Elvis.

"Sure." I immediately felt terrible. It's pretty bad when your own dog has to ask you for water.

We went into the school and found the nearest water fountain. I held the button while Elvis drank. It was a tiny stream of water for such a big dog, so we were there for a while. When we finally got back outside, Alexander and Taisy were waiting for me.

"Hey, guys. Sorry I'm late. Elvis needed a drink of water."

"What time do you have to be home from school?" Taisy asked in a serious tone.

"What? Why?"

"Benj, just answer the question."

"No particular time, I guess. My mom spends most of her afternoons driving the twins around to sports practice. Hey, don't you have practice after school too?"

"Normally I would, but my dad wants me to rest my arm, so I have a few days off. I'm supposed to run the track, but I'm going to skip today."

"Cool. Are you going to walk home with me and Alexander?" I asked.

"Nope, and neither are you. You know why? Because we're going to go get your good luck thingie back."

Alexander piped up, "Benji, I've been trying to reason with her, but she won't listen. And I told her that I don't even know for sure that Billy has it and that what I actually said was that I saw it in the hallway and I *thought* it was Billy's and—"

I shook my head. "No way, nohow, not gonna happen, never, and no thank you."

"See, Benji also understands this is not a good idea," Alexander said. He looked relieved. "Especially since we don't even know for sure he has it. Honestly, a tiny thing like that could be anywhere by now. . . ."

"Nothing ventured, nothing gained. We have no choice but to go for it," said Taisy.

"Taisy, do you even know what you're saying?" I said. "I have a birthday coming up in seven months, and I'd like to live to eleven. I don't think you get it. I spend most of my days avoiding Billy, so if you think I'd go over to *his* house of my own free will, you're totally wrong. So where you say we have no choice, I say we do. And Alexander and I are choosing no."

"Benj, c'mon. Billy's not that bad, and it's not like we're saying you have to go over there alone. We're all going together, as a team, like the Avengers. C'mon, Alexander, don't you want to go on an adventure? Why shouldn't we just go see if he even has it?"

"Alexander, don't listen to her. Tell Taisy this is a bad idea," I said.

It was clear Alexander was stuck in the middle of us. "I honestly don't know what the right thing to do is. I don't think I deserve a vote. Also, I'd like a little more information about what it is we're talking about. When I saw it, it really didn't look all that special, no offense, and so maybe Billy didn't even take it. Maybe someone else picked it up and didn't realize its value and it got accidentally thrown away somehow?"

"It's a titanium lug nut that my dad gave to me when I was five. It's from an actual rocket that went to the moon. My dad's a rocket scientist."

"You know, if my dad gave me something like that, I'd want it back no matter what. My dad said he's going to give me one of his Super Bowl rings someday, and there's no way I'd let anyone take that." Taisy put both hands on her hips. Her mind was clearly made up.

"This isn't a Super Bowl ring. This is a dumb piece of metal that . . ." I trailed off.

I knew I was lying. It wasn't just a dumb piece of metal. I had carried that piece of metal with me every day for the past five years. The truth was, it meant a lot to me, and I wanted it back.

"Fine, it's not a dumb piece of metal. I do want it back," I admitted. "But what are we going to do? Go over there and say, 'Hey, Billy, Alexander has total recall, so he remembers seeing you take it after my medical emergency'?"

"I never said Billy took it. I said—"

Taisy shook her head. "Less talking, more doing! C'mon, this is crazy. Maybe he has it. Maybe he doesn't. But if he has it, we'll get it back. And if he doesn't have it, we'll keep looking. But at least we can say we tried. Life is about trying!"

Man, Taisy sure was good at the locker room speeches. She was starting to convince me, and I was the one who had the most to lose, mainly my face because Billy would surely punch it when I showed up at his house.

"So you really think we should do this?" I looked at Alexander again.

"I'll do whatever you two want to do. And Taisy did promise me if there's an altercation, I won't be expected to fight. My mom always tells me to use my words and not my fists. And if that fails, then I should use my feet instead of my fists, meaning I should run and hide. Taisy also reminded me you do have a two-hundred-pound dog on your side."

Speaking of a two-hundred-pound dog, I was so caught up with Taisy's crazy idea, I'd forgotten about Elvis. I saw him lying in the sun.

"We have to hurry," Taisy said, looking at her watch. "Alexander and I have to be back at school in ninety minutes before our parents pick us up. My dad is picking me up today, and he's never ever late."

"What do your parents think you're doing?" I asked Alexander.

"I usually stay after school and practice music, so they think I'll be doing that. Sometimes I walk home early if I don't feel like staying. My parents know how responsible I am, so they're weirdly relaxed about what I do as long as I'm improving myself in one way or another."

Great, I thought. If I said no, I'd be the chicken of the bunch, but going to Billy's house seemed bat-poop crazy to me. One good thing about not having friends was that I'd never had to deal with peer pressure before.

"Okay, I'm in," I agreed. "Let me go talk to Elvis about what we're doing."

"Did you just say you were going to go talk to your dog?" Alexander looked at me funny.

Uh-oh, busted. Before I could make up an excuse, Taisy stepped in and saved me. "I guess you don't have a dog, Alexander, because I talk to my dog all the time."

"Nope, and I'll never get one. My mom is against anything she thinks will be a distraction from my schoolwork, and that definitely includes dogs."

"I begged my dad for two years before he let me get Princess Daisy, but I finally wore him down."

I walked over to Elvis. "So Taisy thinks we should go over to Billy Thompson's house to see if he has my titanium lug nut."

Elvis didn't respond. In fact, his eyes remained closed.

"Do you think it's crazy? Because I think it's kind of crazy. Maybe I shouldn't go. Maybe I should tell them you're tired and need to go home for a nap."

"I don't need to nap. I'm fine." Wow, he was still definitely mad at me.

"So you think we should go?"

"Why are you asking my opinion? How would you know whether to believe me? You know, with my big furry butt on fire?"

I was about to reply when Taisy said we had to get

going right away.

"Hey, guys, wait up!" I followed Taisy and Alexander to the sidewalk. After a moment, Elvis got up and followed us too.

"So how is it you know where Billy lives?" I asked.

"Alexander saw his address on his backpack once."

Alexander nodded. "He tripped me in the hallway the other day, and when I hit the floor, I landed right next to his backpack. It was written on the side with a black Sharpie."

"And you remember it?"

"That's how total recall works. I remember everything I see. It's 2312 Hamlin Drive."

"Where's that?"

"I don't know." Taisy shrugged. "But Alexander is a human GPS, so I'm following him."

I looked at Alexander. "What's a human GPS?"

Alexander explained that when he found out his family was moving from Philadelphia to the suburbs, he studied a map of the surrounding area. And after Alexander looks at a map once, he has it memorized.

"The fastest route to Billy's would be to take a right on Anderson Lane, left on Piedmont, and then right on Bedford Street, but I'm only allowed to cross the street if there's an actual stoplight and a crosswalk signal, so

I came up with a secondary route where we take a right on Anderson Lane, cross at the light, and go through Brookhaven Park, which will take us to Montgomery Street, where we turn right onto Hamlin Drive. Billy's house is on the south side of the street, so we won't have to cross that street either. It's probably going to add five minutes to our trip, but it will be safer."

Taisy and I looked at each other and started laughing.

"What? What's so funny? Are you laughing at me?"

"We're not laughing at you," I reassured Alexander. "We're laughing because you have one amazing brain. You are a human GPS!"

As we walked through the park together, I thought about how if anyone saw us, we'd look totally normal, just three kids on a sunny day after school walking together in the park, because that's what kids do. Okay, maybe we didn't look totally normal, because the girl was super tall, and the two boys she was with were really short, and maybe from far away people would think she was our babysitter. And Alexander was still dragging his geeky laptop case on wheels (which is not so easy to do on grass, by the way) and oh yeah, we had the biggest dog you've probably ever seen walking right behind us. Okay, thinking about that got my mind off the task at hand for, like, maybe ten seconds. Now I was back to being nervous again.

"Taisy, are you sure this is a good idea?"

"Quit worrying, Benj. It's too late. We're doing it. Besides, aren't you curious about Billy?"

"Not really. In fact, the less I know about him, the better."

Brookhaven Park is popular because it has a huge duck pond in the center of it, where you can rent those paddleboats that are shaped like swans. I'm willing to bet that every single kid in town has a photo of themselves when they were, like, four years old, posing with the bronze statue of four little ducks standing at the edge of the water as if they were about to go in. It's just a thing that people do in our town, a rite of passage. It occurred to me that it'd be pretty funny to get a picture of Elvis with the bronze ducks for my mom's scrapbook.

People also use the pond for their radio-controlled sailboats, and there's even an annual summer radio-controlled sailboat regatta. People come from all over Pennsylvania to race their boats. I've gone a few times with my dad, and every time I watch it, I think that I would really like to get my own radio-controlled boat and compete in the race the next year, but then somehow I never end up doing it. Where does the time go?

It's like my whole youth is just passing me by. I mean, it was only a year ago that I was in the single digits.

When we made it to the edge of the park, I noticed Elvis was still about fifteen feet behind us. He stood with his head cocked to the side.

"Elvis, what's going on?" I asked, and he ran up to me.

"Benji, something's not right. I think there's a problem by the pond."

"What? What do you mean? How do you know? Did you hear something?"

"It's just a gut thing. But I don't know what to do. My instinct says I need to go help, but technically I'm not allowed to leave you. I feel very conflicted right now."

"If someone's in trouble, you gotta go help. I'll be fine. We'll be right behind you."

And *ka-bam*, Elvis took off running toward the pond. He runs really fast for a giant dog. I turned and yelled for Taisy and Alexander. We all ran straight for the pond. Alexander even let go of his laptop case, because it was slowing him down. Just as we got to the top of the hill where we had a view of the pond, Elvis leaped into the water from the bridge that crosses it. There was a massive splash. I'd never seen a dog belly flop before, but that's what he did. I was surprised there was any water left in the pond.

"Look, there's someone in the pond." Taisy pointed. "Do you think they're drowning?"

I'm not a great swimmer myself, though I really like the water. The thought of someone drowning made me woozy. Just thinking of all that murky brown water getting in my ears, going in my mouth and up my nose, stressed me out. And then . . . I fainted.

"Benji, are you okay?" Alexander asked when I woke up seconds later. He looked scared.

"I'm fine, Alexander. I kinda faint when I get really nervous. What's going on with Elvis?"

"I don't know. You fainted, and Taisy ran to the pond to get Elvis, because she thought maybe he needed to save *you* now."

Alexander and I headed down the hill toward the pond, where a small crowd had gathered. We pushed our way through and found Taisy standing next to a very wet Elvis.

"Taisy, what happened?" I asked.

"Are you okay?"

"Yeah, I'm fine. I have a tendency to faint a lot in high-stress situations. You'll get used to it. What happened?"

Before Taisy could answer, a sopping-wet teenager turned to me.

"Is this your dog?"

"It is. Did he save your life?"

"No. In fact, your dumb dog almost caused me to drown. My boat's engine died in the middle of the pond, so I had no choice but to go in there to get it, and out of nowhere something grabbed me by my shirt and started pulling me. I thought it was a shark or an alligator, so I started freaking out, and then I actually did almost drown. And then he dragged me back to the side, and here we all are. So what do you have to say about it?"

"Uh, sorry? I mean, when you think about it, he really didn't mean to scare you. I mean, you could have been drowning, right? I'm sorry if he scared you, though. And I'm also sorry if you have water in your ear, because I know how that feels, and it's a big bummer."

"I'm a lifeguard at the country club, so no, I couldn't have been drowning in the middle of the duck pond."

Elvis looked miserable, and I felt bad for him.

"Hey, what happened to your boat? Did you get it back?" I asked.

As if on cue, the crowd turned their gaze from me

and my giant wet dog to look out at the water, where we all saw the sailboat still bobbing around in the middle of the pond.

"No, I didn't. And you want to know why? Because your dumb dog—"

"Hey, hey, I let the first 'dumb dog' thing go, because you were upset, and sometimes people say things that they don't mean in the heat of the moment." I looked over at Elvis to see if he understood where I was coming from, but he was so miserable, I think my meaning went right over his head. "But now there's no need for any more name-calling. My dog isn't dumb. In fact, he's extremely smart. He could even be smarter than you. But what I was thinking was that since my dog is such a great swimmer, perhaps he could retrieve your boat for you."

I looked at Elvis to see if this was okay. Clearly this was more than okay, because Elvis stood up and walked back into the water and swam toward the boat. The crowd murmured. And the teenager looked at me again.

"Did your dog just understand what you said?"

"I told you he was smart."

We all watched as Elvis swam back out to the middle of the pond and nudged the little blue sailboat back toward the shore. Taisy grabbed my arm with excitement.

"Look! He's not putting it in his mouth, because he doesn't want to wreck it. He's amazing."

I had to admit he was pretty amazing. When he got the boat close enough to the edge, the teenager picked it up. He patted Elvis on the head, and the entire crowd burst into applause. Elvis then did what all dogs do when they are sopping wet. He shook himself, and everyone screamed and ran away.

# 12

"Uh-oh, we're running out of time," Taisy said, looking at her watch. "We've got to leave right now if we're going to make it to Billy's and then back to school on time."

Wow, that Taisy sure was one goal-oriented girl. She was like a dog with a bone that just would not give up.

"Taisy, maybe we've had enough excitement for one day. Elvis is all wet now. Maybe I should get him home and dry him off."

"Yes, I agree. Perhaps we should finish up this mission another day. Who knows—maybe the lug nut will turn up on its own before then. I mean, stranger things have happened," piped up Alexander, who was just back from retrieving his laptop bag. "And the good news is no one took my rolling briefcase! I'm so relieved. Of course now there's grass stuck in the wheels."

Taisy looked at her watch. "We still have forty minutes left. Actually, if you subtract the travel time back from Billy's to the school, we have twenty-five minutes, well, now twenty-four minutes."

I crouched down to help Alexander clean out his wheels. "No one took your rolling briefcase because all the businessmen who would want it are at work right now instead of the park," I joked.

"Hey, my bag is cool. It's made of genuine imitation leather made out of nylon, so it's actually quite light, yet very durable. And I feel that wearing a heavy backpack will stunt my growth."

"What are you talking about?"

"It's not a proven theory, but think about it: walking around with all that weight on your shoulders when your bones are trying to grow taller? I mean, why make your body have to work harder?"

It was kind of the weirdest, most logical thing ever. And boy, did I hope it wasn't true.

"You two, less talk, more walk. Let's go," commanded Taisy.

Taisy led, and Alexander and I followed. I hung

back a little to see how Elvis was doing. By the way: wet dog? Not the best smell in the world.

"I know what you're thinking, and it's not me. It's the pond. I don't even want to know what rancid thing met its untimely demise in that tepid, murky, disgusting water. I really hope I'm up-to-date on all my shots. And I'll most certainly be needing you to draw me a bath this evening."

I guess I was speaking the truth when I said he was smarter than that kid who Elvis thought was drowning but wasn't actually drowning. Elvis was so smart, he knew exactly what I was thinking. "Well, I'm just saying you were pretty amazing in the water back there, and it's not your fault you now smell like a swamp creature on a hot day. And don't worry your big furry head about getting a bath, because there's no way my mom's going to let you sleep in her house when you smell like that," I said, trying to hold back my laughter.

"I just feel foolish. I don't know why I assumed he was drowning. Usually my canine sixth sense is very accurate. It just made no sense that he was out in the middle of the pond when no one else was. And I definitely heard him making unpleasant noises. But I suppose, in hindsight, that was because he was in that awful water. I strongly feel you should write a letter to the parks commissioner to let him know they should drain that pond and refill it with better water."

"Okay, yes, I'll get right on that . . . like, never. But you shouldn't get your collar all in a twist over it just because you made a mistake. It happens to the best of us. Well, it happens to me all the time."

"Well, not to me. I don't usually make mistakes."

"Well, la-di-da. Must be nice, Mr. Fancy-Pants, making such grand big-worded proclamations. Ha, 'proclamations,' that's a big word too. It was a spelling word last week."

"What's that supposed to mean? And by the way, calling a dog Mr. Fancy-Pants really makes no sense, because when's the last time you saw a dog wearing pants, let alone dressy ones?"

"Oh, forget it, I'm tired of arguing with you. Let's just catch up with the others and get this over with." Oh brother, I don't know why I bothered talking to him. Clearly his recent mess-up was just adding to his already bad mood from our fight in the lunchroom. Elvis was not having the best day, and I was sure he was wishing he was frolicking on the White House lawn right about now.

When we finally hit Hamlin Drive, Alexander pointed to a small, run-down brick house at the end of the street. It had a big front yard of brown, overgrown grass. The shades on all the windows were completely drawn, and pieces of the front walk were cracked. I doubted the doorbell even worked. This was just the kind of house I avoided on Halloween.

"So now what? Are we just going to go up and knock on his front door?"

"Do you always ask this many questions? It's not like I have a whole plan figured out." I could tell by Taisy's tone that she was tense and a little frustrated with me.

"Yes, I do ask a lot of questions, and as far as a plan goes, maybe now's a good time to come up with one."

"Benj, it's going to be fine. Relax."

Well, relaxing was certainly out of the question, but I was hopeful she was right about the everything-being-fine part. I had no choice but to follow Taisy as she walked up the front yard, straight up the steps to the door, where she pushed the bell. I was surprised when it rang.

"I guess my plan was pretty much on the money, though you rang the bell when I had suggested knocking, but it's pretty much the same thing, don't you . . ." I looked at Alexander. "I'm babbling, aren't I? I do that when I'm nervous."

Alexander told me that he ran through the state capitals when he was nervous. Or he listed all the presidents of the United States in order. Or, if he really wanted a challenge, he listed them alphabetically by last name, which he felt distracted his brain from whatever it was he needed to distract it from. Okay, clearly I wasn't the only oddball of the group. I held my breath while we waited to see if anyone was home.

"Okay, too bad. No one's home. We should go now. We tried. Good effort, team. We'll get 'em next time," I said, speaking in Taisy's language.

Alexander agreed. "And I second that motion. Should we vote now? All in favor of going home, say 'aye'!" Alexander and I both said aye.

"Wait, maybe he's in the backyard," Taisy suggested, ignoring us both.

"Taisy, that's trespassing. We can't just go snooping in someone else's backyard."

Alexander agreed with me. I turned to Elvis. He was still sulking. "Do you think it's okay to go in the backyard?"

"Well, if the point of all this is to find him, then yes, the backyard would be a good place to start, especially as that's where he most likely is."

"How do you know?"

"Well, someone is back there. I hear music. Unfortunately, we're still a bit too far for me to get a good smell of him. Of course, my own odious pond smell is getting in the way too."

"Odious?"

"It's a fancy-pants way of saying yucky."

I nodded. "You hear music? I don't hear anything."

"Are you talking to your dog again?" Alexander whispered.

"Uh, yeah, it's another one of my habits."

Alexander nodded. "I can see why talking to a dog might be beneficial at times, especially since they can't ever disagree with you."

I nodded back and laughed to myself. If only Alexander knew the real story.

"Wait a second," Taisy whispered, and closed her eyes. "I think I hear something."

I'll say one thing about Taisy, she was one gutsy girl. She walked right around the house on her own. Alexander and I had no choice but to hurry to catch up with her. When we rounded the corner, we all stopped suddenly.

Billy had a huge backyard. It was completely overgrown with grass and weeds that were so tall, they came up almost to my knees. Walking across the yard made me feel like we were walking through the wilderness instead of the suburbs, and I suddenly got nervous about the possibility of wild animals hiding among the weeds, just waiting to pop out. Not that there are many wild animals around here, but you never know. At the very back of the yard, there was a large wooden garage. The roof was caved in on one side. All of a sudden I heard the music too.

"This is a bad idea. We should leave. I don't want to be here anymore," I said, but Taisy was already halfway across the yard, heading straight for the garage. I turned to Alexander. "You know, if we banded together, it would be two against one. Who died and made her team captain of our world?"

"Well, as far as team captain of the world? I'd rather it be her than me or you. No offense, but she's kind of a natural. Plus I'm sort of having fun."

"You are?"

"Benji, let me explain my life to you. I go to school. I study. I do flash cards. I practice the piano, and then I practice the violin. I do more studying, and then more flash cards. I get to watch a half hour of television on the weekdays and one and a half hours of television on weekends. And I've recently been signed up for tennis lessons, so my dad is showing me videos of Wimbledon champion tennis players who can serve at over a hundred miles an hour. Pretty boring, right? Right. But what's worse is that as cool as this total recall thing I have may sound to you, it's also a huge pain in my butt. Mainly because I can remember every single boring day I have down to the tiniest detail, whether I want to or not. And trust me, I've had a lot of days that were totally forgettable, and I'm stuck with them."

I thought about the fact that I'd had my share of boring days myself. Lately, even the hospital was a big snooze fest. You've seen one morgue, you've seen them all.

Alexander continued, "But this day so far, hanging out with you and your dog at lunch, watching your dog save someone from drowning who wasn't even drowning, having a girl like Taisy boss me around? Having you guys think my freaky brain is useful for our super-awesome adventure? Well, this is stuff I only dreamed of doing. And frankly, I don't want this day to end. Ever. But when it does, it may be the first time that I'm truly happy that I will never be able to forget one second of it. Although I really hope you won't be too upset if we don't find your lug nut here, and just because we don't doesn't mean it's actually gone forever. It could always turn up later. Maybe. Hopefully.

Did you know it's a known fact that people who are optimists live longer?"

I looked at Alexander with new eyes. Instead of looking at our extremely dangerous current situation as nerve-racking and scary, which is how I had viewed it, Alexander saw it as the adventure of a lifetime. And he was right. As useful as his brain disorder seemed, there were probably just as many times when it was no fun at all. Maybe Elvis was right. Maybe I did need an attitude adjustment. Maybe I did need a pack of friends to give me a whole new perspective on the world.

"Well, if you're in, I'm in," I said.

Alexander beamed. "Should we make up a secret handshake?"

I smiled back. "Maybe we can work on that later, okay? Right now I think it's best if we try to stay close to Taisy. You know, in case she needs us."

Alexander nodded. "Or in case we need her!"

"Yes, that too." I laughed. And we both took off toward the garage. As we walked through the tall weeds, I wondered if this was why Billy never wore shorts to school. I turned to check on Elvis. His fur was almost dry but now had lots of stuff caught in it. When we rounded the corner of the garage, we found Taisy crouched down, peering into a window. The music was really loud. I put my hand up against the window and felt the glass vibrating.

"It's not good for your eardrums to listen to music that loud," Alexander whispered.

"What did you say?" I whispered back.

He frowned and looked back at me. "What? I can't hear you! What did you say? I don't think we have to whisper, because it's got to be even louder inside."

"What? I can't hear you because the music is so loud!" Now I was practically yelling.

Taisy waved at us to be quiet. I cupped my hands and peered inside too, but the windows were painted completely black. I leaned in and whispered into Taisy's ear this time.

"It sounds like there's a hundred people in there. Those aren't good odds for us."

"I don't think that's actual people. I think it's the music. I think it's a live album. You know, one of those ones where they record a concert," Taisy whispered back. "I think I've heard this record before. My dad listens to it."

Alexander leaned into me. "I've been listening to the words. It's about prison. The song, I mean."

"I don't think it's a good sign when someone paints their windows black and listens to songs about prison.

It means they're hiding something."

Taisy nodded. "I know, and I can't wait to see what it is." And with that she crept along the wall. "I'm going to go look for another window."

Interesting—where I feel someone hiding something means they should have their privacy, Taisy is the opposite. She gets only more determined to discover their secret.

Even though I really wanted to go home, I continued on. I hoped this new spirit of changing my attitude didn't backfire and end badly for me. And by end badly, I mean with me tied up in a garage by a bunch of singing escaped prisoners. As I tried to move, I realized I wasn't going anywhere. Something had me! I turned around and saw Elvis holding on to the back collar of my shirt with his teeth.

"Phew! I'm glad it's just you. What's wrong?"

"What exactly are we trying to accomplish with this particular covert mission? Why aren't we just going up to the garage door and knocking like civilized people?"

"We're trying to see what's going on first. Well, Taisy is. I personally would love to cut bait and leave."

"I can now smell Billy Thompson in there, so why not just knock and politely inquire if he has your lug nut? Also, you should let him know that listening to Johnny Cash this loudly is not good for his eardrums. Why young people insist on listening to music so loud, I'll never know. One of the little girls who lived on the farm played her pop music loudly too. If I had to pick, I'd go with Johnny Cash over pop music any day."

"You know this song?"

Elvis nodded. "It's a classic. 'Folsom Prison Blues' by Johnny Cash."

"Yeah, I don't know that one. It sounds old. C'mon, let's go find them and see what Taisy wants to do next. I'm not in charge."

"No. I guess not. So what you're saying is that Taisy has been designated as the alpha of the group, and so you must go along with her wishes. That makes much more sense. Okay, carry on."

When we rounded the corner, I saw Taisy standing on top of a woodpile stacked along the back wall. She was making her way to a higher window. I've spent a lot of time in emergency rooms, and I've heard of some pretty stupid maneuvers. People standing on top of phone books, which are on top of stools, while wearing high heels to try to change a lightbulb. People climbing out onto roofs to clean out storm gutters. Meaning, lots of bad stuff happens to people when they climb things they aren't supposed to. So I didn't like seeing Taisy up there at all.

"Taisy, come down. It's not safe! You're gonna fall."

"No, I'm not. I was a gymnast. I have awesome balance. One of you come up here so I can boost you up to look into that vent over there."

Alexander took a step forward, but I pulled him back by his shirt. "No way. That's nuts. There's risk and adventure, and there's total stupidity." I looked up at Taisy. "Get down, Taisy. I mean it, or I'm going home right now."

Taisy jumped down from the woodpile. "Sorry, Benj, I didn't mean to scare you."

"Maybe we should just go knock on the door?" I suggested. Everyone nodded, and as we headed around the last corner, we spotted a window that wasn't painted black. The shade was pulled down almost all the way, but there were still two inches on the bottom where we could look in. We all got on our knees, cupped our hands around our eyes, and peered in through the dirty glass.

Now, we couldn't see very much, but the first thing I could make out was one of those bench press weight machines. I recognized it because we have a set in the garage for the twins. Then I noticed something on the floor that completely blew my mind.

"Are you seeing what I think I'm seeing?" I asked Alexander.

"I'm not sure, but if you're seeing what I think I'm seeing, I can see why you're asking me if you're seeing what you're seeing, because I'm still unsure if I'm seeing what I'm seeing. I think."

It had to be fate that Alexander and I had found each other, because weirdly, I understood exactly what he was saying.

Before we could confirm that we were both on the same page, Taisy said exactly what we were both thinking. "Um, am I crazy, or is that part of a leg on the floor over there?"

I nodded my head up and down so hard, I felt my eyeballs shake in their sockets.

"D-d-d-do you think it's real? It can't be real, right?" I asked.

"I don't see any blood," Taisy whispered. "I mean, it can't be real. Billy Thompson may be a lot of things, but there's no way he's the guy who chops off a leg, cleans up all the blood, and then leaves it lying on the floor like it's nothing."

"But maybe that's why he plays his prison music so loudly. So we can't hear the people scream," I said.

"It's definitely not real. I would be able to see it better if someone bothered to clean these windows." For a moment I was relieved. But then I realized that either way, a leg on the floor was weird.

"Okay, it's not real," I whispered. "But how much better is it that there's a fake leg lying there on the floor?"

"Well, at least it's got a cool sneaker on it," said Taisy.

"So let me get this straight," I said. "You're more concerned that the leg lying on the floor has a cute sneaker on it? Seriously? Because I could care less about the sneaker that is attached to the leg that is not attached to a body!"

"I wish I could wear high-top sneakers, but they just don't look right on me. I'm too short." Alexander sighed.

"You guys! Who cares about the stupid shoe! What I want to know is why is there a foot and part of a leg lying on the floor of Billy Thompson's garage? My own feet tingle just looking at it. This has gotten totally creepy. We've got to be at the wrong house. Alexander, are you sure you saw the address right?" I stood up and dusted off my knees.

"I don't make mistakes. This is it. I swear. But maybe this garage isn't Billy's? Maybe they rent it out to someone who likes fake feet and working out?"

"Guys! Guys! Come look!" Taisy waved us back down.

Honestly, I wasn't sure whether I wanted to see anything more. But I got back on my knees, cupped my hands over my eyes, and peered back into the tiny sliver of window. Now there was someone sitting on the bench-press bench, and right next to him was a guitar. But we still couldn't see his face.

"Oh, that's definitely Billy. That's the shirt he had on today," Alexander whispered. "I recognize it because there was a brown stain on the front bottom right that looked like Mr. Peanut."

I looked in, and sure enough, there was a stain on the front in the shape of a peanut wearing a top hat. Just then the person sitting in the chair leaned forward, picked up his left leg, and pulled off his sneaker. Then I saw something really crazy. Where his foot should have been, suddenly there was nothing there at all. Holy moly, I thought, is Billy Thompson so strong that he just pulled off his left foot in his shoe? I didn't even know that was possible. Wait a second, what was I thinking? That wasn't possible. Billy Thompson just removed his entire left foot. And not only did he remove his foot, part of his shin came off with it. Even as I watched it happen, I wondered if it was all just a crazy dream. I felt light-headed. I started to spin. I felt warm.

"Oh man, if he takes off his head next, I'm so out of here!" Alexander said.

And then I fainted.

# 13

When I opened my eyes a few seconds later, Taisy and Alexander were standing right over me. Elvis reached down, grabbed me by my belt buckle, and pulled me back up onto my feet. I was a little wobbly, so he leaned me up against the wall. The song was playing again, but not as loud this time.

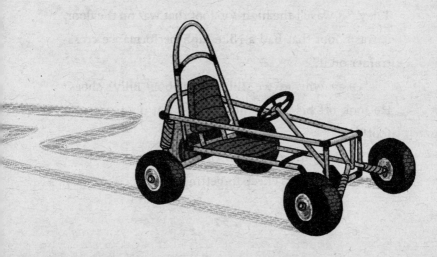

"What did I miss?"

"Billy Thompson plays the guitar," Taisy informed me very matter-of-factly.

Alexander chimed in, "And by the looks of it, he's pretty good. This is a complicated song to play."

For a moment, I wondered if what I'd seen had been all a dream. I tried to speak, but my throat was really dry. "Does anyone have any water?" I asked, and Alexander nodded. He opened his rolling bag, pulled out a flask, and handed it to me.

"A flask?"

"I needed something flat to fit in my bag. Don't worry, it's just apple juice."

"So did I miss anything else besides Billy's musical talents?"

"It got even weirder. We saw Billy put on an entirely different foot, with a totally different shoe on it," said Taisy. "It wasn't the high-top foot that was on the floor, it was a foot that had a Nike high-performance cross-trainer on it."

"Okay, why are we still talking about Billy's shoes? He took off his foot! And then he put on a different foot!"

"With a different shoe."

"Oh right, yes, I keep forgetting about the shoe part.

You know why? Because I was still stuck on the part where he took off his foot! How could we not know that Billy Thompson has a fake foot?"

"Shhhhhhh! Benj, keep your voice down," whispered Taisy.

"I guess he lost his foot somehow and now he wears a prosthetic one, that's all," Alexander said simply. "But I'm guessing it happened to him a long time ago, because you can't tell at all. Maybe he was born like that? Maybe an alligator bit it off? Or a shark? Or maybe he got between an alligator and shark and they were fighting over him," he added excitedly.

"I don't know about all that, but you're right he has no problem walking or running. There's been plenty of times that he's chased me down the hall," I said. "I feel weird about all of this. It's just so surprising. I've never met anyone who was missing a limb. Well, that's not actually true. Once while I was waiting to get an X-ray, I sat next to a guy with only one arm, but he didn't have a fake one, he just had an empty sleeve. Maybe I'm feeling so weird because I'm hungry. I usually have a snack after school when I get home. Does anyone have anything to eat? I think my blood sugar level is getting low. It might make me cranky soon." I sat down against the garage wall.

"Soon? I'd say you were already there." Taisy smiled, and I gave her a look. "What? I just call it like I see it."

Alexander went through his bag again and tossed me something wrapped in tinfoil. "Here—it's from my emergency chocolate stash."

"You have an emergency chocolate stash?"

"It's not for me, it's my mom's. She has me keep it for her, because if she has it in her purse, then she'll eat it all."

I nodded. This made perfect sense to me. I had a feeling my mom and Alexander's mom would get along like gangbusters. I opened up the tinfoil and offered a piece to Taisy.

"I'm not supposed to snack during the day."

"Really? Now's when you're going to start following the rules?"

"Fine." She grabbed a square and popped it into her mouth.

Alexander reached over and broke off a large chunk. "Well, if everybody's ruining their appetite for dinner, then I want some too." He snapped his piece in half. "Here, Elvis, you want a little too?"

And then Alexander tossed a tiny chunk of chocolate in the air toward Elvis. Everything went in slow motion from there. Taisy and I both screamed, "Noooooo!" Taisy dived, and I mean dived, way out, like she was catching a ball between first and second base. Right before the piece landed in Elvis's mouth, she knocked it away with her hand. Then she slammed facedown into the ground. It was pretty unbelievable, and also extremely impressive. Talk about taking one for the team.

"Taisy? Are you okay?" I popped the remaining square into my mouth and rushed to her side. She rolled over when I touched her shoulder, and she was smiling.

"I've still got it!" she said with a laugh.

"If by got it, you mean the crazies, then yeah, you do." I said, now smiling myself. "Alexander, I'm going to need some backup." Alexander and I each offered her a hand. She was so much bigger than us, it took two of us to pull her up. I turned to see Elvis sniffing around the ground.

"Elvis! No. You know you can't eat chocolate!"

Taisy explained to Alexander that chocolate, especially dark chocolate, was poisonous to dogs. Alexander looked upset.

"Oh right, the chocolate milk. I should have remembered. I'm really, really sorry, Benji. I would never have tried to poison your dog on purpose."

"I know that, Alexander. It's no biggie. It was such

a small piece, and besides, Super Taisy saved the day."
I turned to check on Elvis and saw that he had tracked
down the piece of chocolate Taisy had knocked away.
When he looked up at me, I had never seen him more
serious.

"Benjamin, I wasn't going to eat it. I was smelling
it. And my suspicion is unfortunately correct. There
were walnuts in the chocolate."

Uh-oh. This was bad. But I knew he was right,
because I already felt the effects. The tips of my fingers
started to tingle, and my throat felt funny.

Elvis stared at me intently. "Do you have an
EpiPen?"

I nodded. I always carry two at all times, for just
this type of emergency. I am allergic to lots of different things, and I get all types of different reactions.
Sometimes I get hives, sometimes my feet and hands
get puffy, once my entire stomach turned red, but the
worst allergy I have is to walnuts. Walnuts make my
throat close up, which, given the fact that you need to
breathe to live, is not a good thing.

Elvis barked, "Tell Taisy where it is. Now!"

"Taisy, I think we have a big problem." My voice
was a little shaky.

"We sure do," she said.

I turned around to see Billy Thompson standing behind me. He was gripping Alexander and Taisy by their shoulders. He did not look happy, but I held up my hand and stopped him before he could speak.

"The chocolate had walnuts. I'm allergic to walnuts. I have an EpiPen in my backpack. I need it now. Where's my backpack?"

Taisy broke away from Billy's grasp and ran around looking for it. "I don't see it! I don't see it. Alexander, where's Benji's backpack?"

Alexander closed his eyes for a second, and then he opened them again. "He left it at the duck pond."

Elvis took off like a cannon for the park. He barked back at me, "Call Dino!"

"Taisy. Call Dino," I whispered. I was really having problems breathing now, and I dropped to my knees.

Taisy screamed at Billy and pushed him toward me. "Don't just stand there! Go help him!"

"I don't even know what's going on!" Billy helped me sit down on the ground.

"He's allergic to walnuts, and he's going into anaphylactic shock!" Alexander yelled. "He could die."

Taisy screamed at her phone. "Uncle Dino! You have to help us. Benji accidentally ate a walnut and he's sick!"

She must have had him on speakerphone, because I could hear him shouting back at her to calm down and speak slowly.

"Here, look!" She pointed her phone at me, and I saw Dino's face on the screen.

I waved at him weakly. "Hey, Dino."

"Taisy! Isn't there an adult around?"

Taisy looked at Billy. "Are your parents home?"

Billy shook his head. "I don't have a dad, and my mom's working."

"No, there aren't any adults."

"Benji should have an EpiPen with him. I'm going to have to walk you through what you need to do, okay? He'll be just fine in a minute. It's going to be okay."

"He doesn't have it! I mean, he does, but it's in his backpack, and he accidentally left it in the park. Elvis went to go get it. It's not far, and he should be back soon. But what if it's not there? What if someone took it? Tell me what to do! Please."

Alexander knelt down next to me. His brown eyes watered and his face wrinkled up. He was trying not to cry. "His lips are turning blue! I don't think that's a good thing."

I heard Billy shout, "The dog is coming! And he's

got the backpack. He's just across the street. Man, that dog can run!"

Thirty seconds later, Taisy shook my backpack upside down and everything poured out of it. "I can't find it! What does it look like? Is this it?" Alexander ran over to help and opened the front pocket. He pulled out one of the EpiPens and revealed the needle. The universal reaction when kids see needles is total fear. Billy, Taisy, and Alexander all said, "Whoa."

Dino was still on the phone, but I couldn't hear him anymore, mainly because I was on the verge of blacking out. Dr. Helen told me if this ever happened, it was very important to stay calm, because panic only makes everything go faster. I tried to focus on breathing as well as I could through my rapidly closing windpipe.

"So I'm supposed to just stab this into his heart?" asked Taisy. "I don't think I can do it. How will I even know where is heart is through his shirt?"

"What? We're supposed to stab him in the heart? Are you sure? He's not a vampire!" said Billy.

Dino told Taisy that wasn't going to be necessary. All she had to do was jab it in my leg and push the button, which would deliver the medicine.

Taisy tossed the pen to Alexander. "You do it,

Alexander, I don't want to hurt him."

"I can't. I don't want to mess up. Don't you think I've done enough already? I'm the one who did this to him. You do it."

"Give me that. You two are such babies," Billy huffed, and grabbed the EpiPen. "I'll do it."

EpiPens work amazingly fast, and within seconds my throat opened back up and I could breathe again. When I sat up, everyone was sitting on the ground around me. We were all dazed and confused, and all eyes were on me.

"Billy, can I get some water?"

Billy stood up and looked at me. His face showed genuine concern. "Are you okay?"

I nodded. "Thanks for stabbing me in the leg."

"It was kinda fun. C'mon, it's hot out here. Let's go inside—I've got a fan on."

Taisy helped me to my feet, and she and Alexander flanked me as we followed Billy into the garage. It was pretty dim inside except for a rusty floor lamp shining on a music stand with sheet music on it. I walked over and looked: "Folsom Prison Blues" by Johnny Cash. Huh, maybe Elvis does know everything, I thought.

Billy walked over to a minifridge and pulled out a

few bottles of water. I sat on an old couch covered with blankets. Taisy sat next to me, and Alexander sat next to her. Elvis lay down directly at my feet. He was still breathing heavily from his run to the park. We drank in silence. I drank half my bottle and then nudged Elvis with my foot, and he sat up. I offered him the rest of the water, and he lapped it up like he had been lost in the desert.

"So, are you sure you're okay now, Benji? I mean, do you need to go to the hospital?" asked Billy.

I looked up at him. I found it really odd to hear Billy talk to me in a seminice way. I shook my head. "No, I'm okay. Those pens work really fast, and I'm fine. I've had this happen to me a few times, so I kinda know the drill."

"Why were you guys even here?" he asked.

"Ask Taisy," I said.

"Ask Alexander," she said.

Since Alexander didn't have anyone else to pass the buck to, he tried to explain to Billy why we'd come here, but first he started with the fact that he has total recall.

Billy scowled. "I don't care about any of that. Why were you sneaking around like that? Why didn't you just knock on the garage door?"

"Because we're all scared of you," I said.

"So why are you even here then?"

"Do you have my lug nut? Alexander said he saw you with it in the hallway after my episode. It's really important to me. My dad gave it to me. It's kind of my good luck charm. And as you can see, I'm a kid who needs all the good luck I can get."

"You think I took your lug nut? Why would I want it?"

"Why isn't anyone listening to me?" said Alexander. "I never said I saw Billy with it! I said I saw it and that I assumed it was Billy's."

"That's basically the same thing, Alexander, and when are you ever wrong?" asked Taisy.

"It's not at all the same thing. When you assume something, that means that you could totally be wrong. Actually, my mom says a funny thing about the word 'assume,' and I would share it, but I can't because it involves a word that I'm not allowed to use. And by the way, I'm wrong a lot. Don't you recall what just—"

Before Alexander had a chance to continue, Taisy leaped up from the couch. She pointed at an old cuckoo clock on the wall in the corner.

"Is that the right time?!"

Billy nodded. "Yeah, why?"

"Oh no, oh no, no, no, no, no! This is bad. We have to go. Right now. We're going to be late, and if I'm not back at school when my dad shows up, he's going to get really mad, and you do not want to see my dad get mad. I already had to beg my uncle not to rat me out. I'm not even supposed to be here. I'm supposed to be running laps on the track. Why is everyone just sitting there looking at me? I said we have to go now. Billy, give Benji back his lug nut thingie right now."

"I don't have it."

Alexander stood up from the couch. "Okay, well, that's that. Sorry to have bothered you."

I stood up too. "Why should I believe you when you lie all the time at school?"

"Are you calling me a liar?" Billy took a step toward me. I tried to back up, but instead I just sat back down on the couch.

I looked up at him and calmly said, "Yes, but I'm not only calling you a liar, I'm calling you a thief too. Now give it back."

"I don't care about any of this. We need to go. I can't be late. You don't understand what will happen to me if my dad finds out I left the school. It won't be good. It'll be bad." Taisy grabbed Alexander and dragged him toward the door. "Now, now, now! We're never going to make it back in time. I'm so dead. This is a nightmare!"

"Stop screaming, Taisy. If you need a ride, I can get you back to school in less than five minutes," said Billy.

Taisy stopped in the doorway and turned around. I noticed that her bottom lip was quivering. "Don't joke around, Billy. This is really serious."

"I have a go-kart. It'll fit everyone. Well, except for Benji's fat dog."

"Hey! He's just big boned."

Alexander was shaking his head. "I don't think that's a good idea. I don't think my mom would want me to ride in a go-kart."

"Did your mom ever say you couldn't ride in a go-kart?" Taisy asked, pushing Alexander out the door.

"No."

"Then technically you're not doing anything wrong. I've got to get back to school on time. And if Billy can get me there, then we're doing it. Billy, you can take me and Alexander first. Benji will stay here and rest, and then you can come back and take him home."

Billy looked at me. "Is she always this bossy?"

I nodded. But as much as I wasn't thrilled at the idea of hanging around Billy's secret garage, I wasn't sure if the go-kart was a good idea either.

"Do you have a helmet?" I asked Billy.

"Maybe I do, maybe I don't. Who wants to know?"

"Who wants to know? I want to know! That's why I'm asking you. Billy, drop the tough act. We don't have time for it. So just be nice. Do you have a helmet or not?"

"I guess I might have a few lying around."

We all went outside, and Billy walked around to the back of the garage, where he pulled a tarp off a pretty decent-looking two-seater go-kart. I couldn't help it, I was impressed by the secret life of Billy Thompson. Guitar playing, weight lifting, able to remove his foot, and now a builder of go-karts. I guess I had pictured him throwing rocks at stray dogs when he wasn't at school.

"Did you build it yourself?"

"Yeah, with a little help from my mom's boyfriend. I used a riding lawn mower engine. Let's just say my mother's not too happy with me right now, because as you can see, our grass hasn't been mowed in a while."

Wow. Billy was almost like a normal kid, talking about his mom being mad at him. I never really thought about Billy having a mom at all. He climbed in behind the steering wheel. Taisy and Alexander squeezed in next to him and put on their helmets.

Billy put his foot on the gas, and they roared out of his yard. It was a bumpy ride. I wasn't sure I'd risk my own life riding with Billy Thompson, so I wasn't too happy at the thought of my friends riding with him. Now that I had friends, I kind of wanted to keep them. Alive.

# 14

I couldn't believe it. I was alone at Billy Thompson's house. Though I guess being out in his dumpy garage was hardly the same as being inside his real house. I wondered if Elvis and I should walk home. But I also still felt a little woozy. This had truly been one of the most bizarre days ever. I sat back down on the couch and closed my eyes.

After a few seconds, the image of Billy taking off his foot popped back into my head. Was that really what we'd seen? With all the excitement of my near-death experience, we hadn't had time to talk about anything. I stood up and looked around. I know it's not polite to snoop around other people's private stuff, but then again, Billy wasn't exactly polite all those times he terrorized me at school either.

"Where are you going?"

I looked at Elvis, who was all stretched out on the floor.

"I thought you were asleep."

"Nope. Just resting."

"Okay, well I'm going to look around a bit."

I found a dusty old lamp in the corner and pulled the rusty chain. The lightbulb blinked on, and I could now see the garage was pretty big. And it was was a total mess. Bed frames, plywood, steel shelves filled with magazines and what looked like old auto parts. The only thing that looked kind of new was a steel cabinet on the far right wall. There was a padlock on it, but it was open and just hanging there, and the cabinet door wasn't even shut all the way. Honestly, at this point, on this particular day, I wouldn't have been surprised by anything I found in there. Jars of eyeballs, snow globes, an Easy-Bake Oven? Maybe even my lug nut, but I doubted it. That would be too easy.

I pushed the door open with my foot, and well, I was wrong. I could still be surprised. Inside the cabinet were lots of different-size legs and shoes all lined up on two shelves. They were arranged by size, and inside each different shoe was a foot, and part of a leg. Some of the legs looked like actual fake legs with fake flesh-colored skin, but most of them were metal legs, like something you would see on a futuristic robot. I reached in and picked up the one with the black and green high-top sneaker on it with the metal leg.

"When I was four years old, I was in a terrible car accident with my parents."

I froze. So much for Elvis being a watchdog. Billy was back. I slowly put the foot in the cabinet and closed the door. Then I turned to face Billy Thompson.

"My dad was in a band. Well, he was really a UPS delivery guy, but he sang in a band on the side. They usually didn't bring me along when he had a gig, but one night the babysitter had the flu, so they had no choice but to take me."

Billy paused and looked at the sheet music on the stand. For a moment, I thought he was going to cry. Out of all the crazy things that had happened that day, this was by far the craziest. Billy Thompson was a real kid, with real feelings, and he seemed to love his dad as much as I loved mine. I was stunned. My mouth was probably hanging wide open. Billy just kept talking.

"It was snowing when we left. And when we were driving home, we hit a patch of ice. Our car started spinning like crazy right into the oncoming traffic lane. I woke up in the hospital two days later after two surgeries that I didn't even know about. And that's how I lost my left foot and part of my leg. So now I wear different prosthetics, and that's where I keep my different shoes and legs."

"You can't even tell, though," I said.

"No duh, that's the whole point. Why would I want anyone knowing? It's no one's business but my own. I don't let it stop me from doing anything. And I don't want anyone to know about it, so you better not blab it to anyone at school. Or else."

"You know, you could try asking nicely instead of threatening me all the time. And for your information, I'm not going to say anything to anyone."

"Okay, don't tell anyone. Please. If you know what's good for you."

I smiled. "Well, that's a little better. That was half asking and half threat, but I'll take it. I won't say anything. I swear. Is that your dad's guitar that you were playing, the one from that night?"

"Yeah, how did you know?"

"I didn't know for sure—it was just a hunch."

"My mom says it took the firemen an hour with the Jaws of Life to get me out of the car, it was so crunched up in the crash. The whole thing was totaled, but my dad's guitar made it out without a scratch on it. My mom makes me play my music out here, because she thinks I play too loudly. But I think it makes her sad, because it reminds her of my dad."

"Yeah, my mom makes me keep my music down too." Actually, I don't really play music all that much, and when I do, I listen to it with earphones on from my iPod.

"Sometimes I feel like I know more about my dad, and he's not even around, than I know about my mom. She works a lot, and she's pretty quiet. My dad was the loud one."

"It's the opposite with my parents. My mom's definitely the loud one. So loud everyone seems quiet next to her."

Billy nodded. "Yeah, I've seen her around a lot at school. She is loud."

I made a face, because there's kind of a rule that I

can talk bad about my mom, but no one else can. "She's around a lot because she's a little overprotective when it comes to me. I was sick a lot as a baby," I said.

This time Billy didn't respond, and I honestly didn't know what to say anymore myself. This was by far the longest conversation I'd ever had with Billy Thompson. After a while, I finally blurted out, "I should get going. But I can walk if it's a pain for you to drive me."

"I'll take you. Of course, I'm going to have to hitch up a wagon to the back of the go-kart for your giant dog. Give me a second."

Billy jerry-rigged an old rusty red wagon to the back of the go-kart with some twine and duct tape. Elvis and I sat inside the garage, watching through the window. I had pulled up the shade to let some more light in. All the dust that came off it made both me and Elvis sneeze.

"If you think I'm riding in that red thing, you are sadly mistaken," Elvis said.

"Fine, you can ride up front with him, and I'll ride in the wagon."

"Forget it—I don't have the energy to save your life again when that thing breaks off on the first hill we climb and you go rolling into traffic. I'm fast, but I'm not that fast."

"Speaking of, I haven't had the chance to say thank you for saving my life earlier. Thanks for getting the backpack."

"You shouldn't be thanking me—you should be punishing me. I can't believe I didn't notice you left it behind. I'm a disgrace to the service dog profession. So it is I who owe you the apology for that particular incident. Maybe I was still mad at you for all the harsh things you said to me at lunch. No one has ever called me a liar before. Do you think we should talk about it some more so we can understand what exactly we both were feeling?"

"Or how about just call it even Steven and be done with it? I don't know about you, but I don't have the energy to fight with you or to talk about my feelings. I just want to get home and lie in the air-conditioning and eat a snack."

Elvis wagged his tail. "No kidding, you and me both."

Billy banged on the window when he was done, which made us both jump back. Elvis snorted, "That kid really has appalling manners."

"Don't make fun of him—he's had a tough life."

"Pish-posh, Benjamin, what you will soon find out is that everyone has a tough life. What counts is how you handle your unfortunate circumstances. It's called character, and I'm trying to build yours up, but you already have a pretty decent foundation. This Billy kid, he's trouble. I can smell it. Just because he's had to deal with lots of hardship doesn't mean he has the right to make other people's lives hard too."

"He did save my life when he injected me with the EpiPen."

"I'm the one who brought it to you, and I would have injected you, but I don't have thumbs. And I watched him when he did it, and he looked like he almost enjoyed sticking it to you."

Elvis and I walked outside. Billy had done a pretty good job of securing the wagon to the back of the go-kart.

"Are you sure it's safe?"

"Sure I'm sure. Don't be such a baby!"

"I'm not a baby, I'm just saying I don't know if I can get him to sit in there. He may not even fit. It looks too narrow for his, uh, big-boned bottom."

"Fine, you sit in there then. He can ride shotgun with me. C'mon, let's get a move on. I have some chores to do before my mom gets home."

"Elvis, get up front. I'm going to ride in the back."

I noticed that Billy had made a seat belt for the back with some nylon straps. "You promise you won't drive too fast?"

"Just shut up and get in already. Why are you so whiny?"

And there he was, the old Billy. I guess some things never really change.

"Do you want to just walk? Because I'm fine with that too, though you could have told me you were going to weenie out before I used up all my duct tape."

"I'm not weenieing out!"

"Then get in."

No one makes me angrier than Billy Thompson. He makes me feel powerless, which I hate. I climbed into the red wagon. Elvis just stared at me and shook his head.

"Elvis, get in. I'm back here because of you anyway."

The ride was terrifying, exhilarating, scary, extremely bumpy, loud, and very much like a roller coaster at the amusement park, except that it lasted much longer than the typical minute and a half. Billy was a pretty good driver, and most of the streets had sidewalks. When we were only a few blocks from my house, Billy turned down a side street.

"Billy! What are you doing? I live three blocks straight ahead."

"I think we're being followed," he said in a low voice.

I started to look around, but he said sharply, "Don't turn around. I don't want them to know we know."

"What do you mean we're being followed? Billy, are you playing a joke on me? Seriously, I really just want to go home." Elvis turned around and gave me a look. "Elvis, is he serious?"

"Dude, did you just ask your dog a question?"

Elvis barked, "It's true. We are being followed. And you should tell your rude friend that if this stupid go-kart had a passenger rearview mirror, it would be more helpful."

"Dude, did your dog just answer you?" Billy stepped on the gas, and we took off again. He drove crazy fast for the next two blocks and then made a sharp right turn, which almost flung me out of the wagon. I was gripping so hard my hands hurt. Billy finally lurched to a stop behind some tall hedges.

"Okay, party's over. Get out."

"You think someone is following us, and you're just going to dump us on the side of the road?"

"Yup. Plus I gotta get home. So vamoose."

I would never understand this kid, ever. I loosened the nylon straps along my legs and stepped out of the wagon. Of course, my right leg had fallen asleep, and when I tried to stand on it, I lost my balance and fell over in the yard. Elvis picked me up pretty quickly, but there was no way Billy didn't see it. "Well, thanks for the ride."

"Yeah, whatever. You owe me gas money now. I'll collect later. And I'm not lying. I don't have your dumb lug nut thingie."

This time I believed him. Maybe Alexander was right.

"Okay, Billy. I'm sorry I accused you. That was wrong of me. And I also want to say maybe you're not as mean as I thought you were. Okay, you're not that nice, but maybe it's not your fault. I mean, it is kind of your fault, because you don't really have to pick on kids who are weaker than you, but maybe you do it because your own life has been pretty sucky. I'm really sorry that your dad died."

Billy laughed. Okay, again, not the response I was expecting from him. "My dad didn't die in the accident. He still lives in Michigan. My parents got divorced last year, and my mom and I moved here to be closer to my granddad." All of a sudden he was serious again. "But just because I told you about my dad, don't think we're friends. Or that you really know anything about my life. Sure I may only have one foot, but I'm still faster, stronger, and cooler than you and your two feet. The only days you should feel bad for me are when it's really hot out, because I don't like to wear shorts. Later."

Billy hit the gas and took off. I heard him laughing all the way down the street. I just shook my head. I was pretty sure singing prison songs would come in handy for him one day.

As soon as he was gone, a large black SUV pulled over right in front of us. Elvis leaped into action and dragged me back five feet from the sidewalk into someone's yard. He then stood in front of me. The tinted window rolled down. We were being followed by . . . Taisy!

"Hey, guys! I thought that was you two. Of course, it's pretty hard to miss a giant dog riding a go-kart. It's not really a sight you see every day. Anyway, I have Princess Daisy with me. Can she meet Elvis now? See, Daddy? Do you remember Elvis from the hospital two days ago?"

"Yes, Taisy, he is a good-looking dog," I heard Taisy's dad say inside the car. Elvis beamed. I've never met a dog who loves being fawned over more.

Taisy got out of the car, leaving the door wide open.

"So do you want to meet Princess Daisy?"

"Sure, I'd love to meet Princess Daisy. Where is she?" I asked, turning my head toward the open door.

I was expecting Princess Daisy to get out of the world's largest SUV, but instead she popped out of Taisy's purse just like a piece of toast. She was a tan French bulldog with a little bit of Chihuahua in there, and she was very cute. On her pink blinged-out collar there was a daisy that was almost as big as her whole head. She just sprang out of Taisy's bag straight up into the air, and instinctively I put my hands out and caught her. I sorta wished the twins were around to see it, because whenever they throw anything at me that I'm not expecting (like all the time), I'm always surprised and drop it. I have bad hand-eye coordination, bad reflexes, bad grip, bad timing, and well, you get what I'm saying.

But I caught Princess Daisy. She licked my face, and I laughed because it tickled. This was when Taisy leaned in so close I could smell her strawberry lip gloss. She whispered, "We made it back two minutes before my dad showed up. Billy's a really good driver. It was super fun." She then straightened up and said in her regular voice, probably more for her dad's benefit than my own, "She likes you, and Princess Daisy is very picky about who she likes and who she doesn't."

Taisy sounded happy, and I was happy that Taisy was happy, and I was really happy she and Alexander hadn't gotten into any trouble while helping me try to get my lug nut back. I couldn't believe that just twenty minutes ago Taisy was losing it and biting everyone's head off, and now she was back to being super-girlie-sweet Taisy. It was like a female Dr. Jekyll and Ms. Hyde scenario, big-time. Then I noticed Princess Daisy's tiny little nails were painted pink. I looked at Taisy in surprise.

"What?" she said. "Just because I'm better than most boys in sports doesn't mean I can't be girlie too. Girls are very complicated, Benji. That's what makes us so special."

I shrugged. She'd get no lip from me on the subject. I had already learned from my mom how complicated women can be. All this time Taisy's dad was checking out Elvis, and finally Elvis must have smelled Princess Daisy (she smelled like a warm peach pie, by the way), and he came over.

So my mom watches a lot of those mushy movies. She says there's nothing better than chocolate and a movie about love. Because I'm sick and home a lot,

I've seen a lot of them with her. I can't say I like them as much as she does, because I'm not a girl, but I will admit that sometimes I understand why she likes them. I guess my favorite part about them is the guaranteed happy ending. I also like slow motion, and they do that a lot in those types of movies. Sometimes I feel like life just goes by too quickly, and I wish that I had a master remote control button where I could just slow things down and watch them again, kinda like that time when Elvis was flying through the morgue on that steel table.

Well, every now and again in real life, you see things in slow motion. I'm not saying it's happened to me all that often, and maybe it only happens when it's about true love . . . but when Elvis saw Princess Daisy, I swear I looked up to see if there were any cartoon bluebirds circling above his head. He glanced over at me, looked away, and then did a double take so fast I'm surprised he didn't get whiplash. It's like he looked over and saw boring old Benjamin and then he looked away, but then his brain caught up with his eyes and he was like, wait, what was that in his arms? And then he looked again.

His jaw dropped when he saw Princess Daisy. Seriously, his mouth opened, and a big old strand of drool fell right out. Probably not the best first impression, but at least it was sincere. When Elvis came bounding over to say hello, that's when it was like slow motion. I saw every strand of hair on his long, fluffy coat, and he whipped his head around, which caused his drool to go flying out of his mouth, and suddenly everyone was ducking for cover. Taisy, because she has amazing reflexes, ducked and managed to miss the flying spit. I wasn't so lucky, as I caught a big glob right above my left eye. Gross.

Then suddenly Elvis was face-to-face with Princess Daisy, and he sat very politely and was very still. I held out Princess Daisy so she could sniff Elvis, and it seemed she approved, because she wagged her tail in my arms.

"She likes you," I said.

Taisy scooped Princess Daisy out of my arms and put her on the ground next to Elvis. Trust me, no two dogs could look more different. Princess Daisy was pretty much the size of one of Elvis's paws. Taisy said she thought Princess Daisy liked Elvis. And I told Taisy I thought Elvis more than just liked Princess Daisy. Then we both got embarrassed, and luckily, we were saved by Taisy's dad, who got out of the car and came over to say it was time for them to go.

It was hard to separate Elvis from Princess Daisy, but Taisy had a meeting with one of her private coaches. I said I had to go too, not because I had anything important to do, but because if I didn't get home soon, my mom would probably call in the SWAT team to come find me. Everyone laughed. I almost said that I was being totally serious, but I decided to just let it go.

The last four blocks to home, Elvis was floating on air. If a dog could hum, Elvis would have. I was about to tease him, but then I realized I hate getting teased myself. And why should I tease him anyway? So what if he liked Taisy and Princess Daisy? I liked them too.

# 15

Elvis and I rounded the corner to my house, and I saw two black sedans out front, one parked in the driveway and the second one parked on the street. It looked really odd, so we stopped and stared. Elvis took one glance at the license plates and told me they were definitely Secret Service cars.

He nudged me forward, and pretty soon we were running toward the house. When I got up to the door, a man opened it before I had a chance to. I was out of breath from running, my heart pounding. My mom was serving cake and tea in our living room to three men with black suits on. Not a single one of them smiled.

"Benji, are you okay? Why are you late from school?" my mom asked.

"I'm fine, Mom. I'm late because . . . well, uh, we ran into Taisy and her dad on the street, and Taisy wanted her dog, Princess Daisy, to meet Elvis. I think Elvis is in love with Princess Daisy. I could tell, because it looked like one of those lovey-dovey mushy movies you watch on TV where people see each other and it's love at first sight, but this time it was the doggy version."

When I'm nervous, I talk too fast and too much, and it was worse in this case, because I was only telling a half-truth. It was true that we'd run into Taisy and her dad, but I conveniently left out the part where Elvis saved a nondrowning man, we went to Billy's house, and oh yeah, how I almost died when I ate a walnut by accident.

"What? Who is Taisy? Who is Princess Daisy?"

"Taisy is the girl we met at the hospital, remember? And Princess Daisy is Taisy's dog. But she's not a real princess. It's just a fake title."

My mom, even though I could tell she was nervous

too with all these strangers in her living room, couldn't help but beam at me. She's always telling me I need to make some friends. She never said anything about it directly, but I guess it made her sad that I never talked about anyone from school.

"Well, why don't you come and have some cake and tell me all about it?" she said.

"Or . . . maybe you could tell me who all these guys wearing dark suits are?" I said, nodding at the men.

"Oh right! Benji, this is Secret Service Agent Daniels and his friends." A short, stocky man walked up to me and held out his hand.

"Hello, Benjamin, I'm Agent Daniels. I work for the president of the United States."

"Hello, Mr. Daniels. I'm ten years old and in the fourth grade. I'm too young to work, so I don't work for anyone."

Everyone laughed. Before I could say anything else, a yellow Labrador came bounding into the room from the kitchen, straight for me. I panicked and threw my arms up to protect my face. I was sure I was about to be knocked over, and hard. But at the last second Elvis intervened and knocked the other dog away.

"Whoa. Elvis. Easy there, it's okay," I said.

The other dog lay on the floor, eyeing Elvis suspi-
ciously.

"Mom, what's going on?"

"Well, Benji, it turns out you were right. There was
a mix-up, and Elvis really was the president's dog like
you said. This is your normal-sized dog. His name is
Ripley."

I turned to Ripley. He was panting and happy. I
walked up to him and held out my hand.

"Hi Ripley. I'm Benji." Ripley barked happily and
licked my hand. Well, one thing was for sure. Ripley
didn't talk. Well, not in a way that I understood. I petted his head, and he happily started licking my face. I
noticed that Elvis looked very tense.

"So what does this mean?" I asked.

"Well, Benji, it means that we're here to take Elvis to
the White House, and Ripley is going to stay here with
you," said Agent Daniels with his mouth full of cake.

"Oh." I wasn't sure what to say. I didn't know
exactly how I felt. "So when is this happening?"

My mom came quickly to my side, putting her arm
around me. "Benji, honey, I think it's happening now.
It's time for you to say good-bye to Elvis."

"Oh." I still didn't know what to say. I looked over
at Elvis, and he looked as sad as I was.

"So that's it? You're just taking Elvis right now and I'm never going to see him again?"

Agent Daniels looked at his colleagues and then at my mom. Clearly, he was not a guy who was used to answering to a ten-year-old.

"Well, perhaps we could work out a visit if your family ever comes to DC. I'd say you could write emails, but he is just a dog." Agent Daniels chuckled, but he was the only one who laughed.

"Elvis is much more than just a dog. He could write emails. If he could type."

No one laughed. "That was a joke," I said, and everyone chuckled awkwardly.

"Well, Mrs. Barnsworth, thank you for the amazing cake," said Agent Daniels. "But we should really hit the road. We've got a long drive ahead of us."

Suddenly it all sank in. My throat tightened and my stomach hurt.

"Wait, I, uh, can I have a little time alone with Elvis to say good-bye? In private?"

Everyone looked at one another. My mom spoke up. "Benji, why don't you and Elvis go upstairs to your room, and you can get his stuff. I'm sure he'd like to take some of the toys we bought him."

Agent Daniels looked at his watch and sighed.

"You can wait another five minutes, can't you?" My mom said it like a question, but her tone said otherwise. Even Secret Service Agent Daniels didn't want to say no to my mom.

"Sure. Of course. We'll wait down here."

"C'mon, Elvis, let's go upstairs." I walked up the stairs, and Elvis followed me. Ripley got up to follow too, but Elvis turned and barked at him. Ripley lay back down again. I had never seen Elvis so stern. It was the longest climb up the stairs of my whole life. By the time we got to my room, I was doing everything I could not to cry. When I closed the door to face Elvis, I didn't know what to say.

"Wow. So, uh, wow."

"Benjamin. I, uh . . ." Elvis didn't know what to say either.

"I'm sorry I called you a liar earlier at school. I didn't mean it. I believed you. I was just mad. And I know you were telling the truth."

"It's okay. I knew you were upset. I'm sorry I pushed you so hard about Alexander."

"No, you were right. Like always. I was just stubborn. Or scared. I guess I am a coward."

"No, you're not. You're the bravest kid I know. And I had a wonderful time here."

"Yeah?"

"Absolutely."

"I'm glad. But now you're going to go live that extraordinary life you've been wanting to live. Which is cool. I mean, the White House has lots of grass."

"Yes, it does."

I couldn't pretend anymore. I didn't want him to go. The tears poured out of me, and there was nothing I could do to stop them.

"Please don't cry, Benjamin." Elvis walked up to me and licked them away. I threw my arms around his big furry neck and buried my face in his hair.

"I'm going to miss you so much! You will always be my first and favorite dog."

"Well, you'll always be my first master. It's going to be okay."

"Yeah. Ripley seems nice."

"Yeah, for a Lab. I mean, yes, I'm sure he's a great dog. And he'll look after you. Not like I would look after you, but I'm sure he'll be fine."

"I'm sorry you won't have a chance to say good-bye to Taisy and Princess Daisy and Alexander."

"Yeah, me too. You tell them I said good-bye, okay? And be careful around that Billy kid from now on. I really don't trust him. And make sure Ripley minds his manners."

"Okay. I'll tell Ripley you have dibs on Princess Daisy."

Elvis chuckled, but I could tell he was really hurting inside too.

"So is this good-bye?"

"I think it's good-bye for now. But not forever. Maybe you can come and visit me at the White House. And if you write letters, I'm sure someone will read them to me. I hope."

"Okay."

There was a light knock on my door, and then my mom came in.

"Hey, baby, you okay?" She looked at my tearstained face. I wiped my nose on my sleeve.

"Yeah, Mom. I'm just sad. I really love Elvis. I wish he didn't have to go."

"I know, honey. And Elvis, it was a real honor to have you with us." She bent down and hugged Elvis too. She held up a brown paper bag. "I went to the butcher today and bought you some beef bones that I boiled up for you. Maybe you can take them on the road for a snack?"

Elvis licked her face in response.

I went over to my desk drawer and pulled out a bag of Doritos that I had stashed there. "Here, Mom, let's put these in there for him too." She opened the bag and I placed the Doritos inside.

"Think of us when you eat Doritos, okay? I'm sure you'll have plenty at the White House."

"No, after this bag I won't eat them anymore. Doritos are our thing. We'll eat them together the next time I see you." Wow, who knew that Elvis was as mushy as one of those movies?

"Mom, do you think we can go to the White House and visit Elvis? Or was Agent Daniels just full of it?"

"Benjamin, that's not nice. I'm sure he meant what he said. I'll bring it up again. I don't see why we can't go and visit. Maybe in the summer."

The summer was still a long way off. And the thought of it made me start crying again. I hated Elvis to remember me as a big crybaby, but my mom has always said that it's okay to cry. It just means you feel something strongly, and it's better to feel a lot than to feel nothing at all.

"So we should probably go downstairs. I think they're waiting for us."

"Okay. One more minute, Mom. I promise we'll be

right down." My mom nodded and left the room.

I wished I knew what to say.

"Elvis, I guess I should call you by your formal name now, Parker—"

"No, you can call me Elvis. I like it. Coming from you."

"I just want you to know that you changed my life. Seriously, I think I made some new friends today, and I wouldn't have made them without you. Of course, with you gone, they might not be interested in me anymore."

"That's not true, Benjamin. I just helped you find your pack, that's all. You're a great kid. You're the best kid I know."

"I'm the only kid you know."

"That's not true. I know Taisy and Alexander now."

"You like me better than Taisy?"

"Of course I do. Though I think she's cuter. And you have a bad haircut."

I laughed. "Well, anyway. Thanks. And I'm sorry I called you uptight."

"You never called me uptight."

"Oh, right. Well, I thought it. I just didn't know you all that well."

I hugged him one more time. Hard.

"I guess we should go now," I said, not really meaning it.

"Yep. Agent Daniels is probably pacing downstairs. Talk about uptight—if you look up the word in the dictionary, I bet you'd see his picture."

"Yeah." I laughed despite myself.

Neither of us made a move. It was too painful to think about walking out of the room, because that meant he was really leaving.

Elvis walked over to my bedroom window and put his paws up on the windowsill. I walked over and joined him.

"What are you doing?"

"I'm thinking, too bad your room is on the second floor, because if it wasn't, I could toss you into some bushes and we could run away together."

I knew he was joking, but I appreciated that the thought had crossed his mind, because I gotta be honest, it was exactly what I was thinking too.

My mom came in again. "Benjamin, Agent Daniels is about to blow a gasket down there, so I think it's time for Elvis to go."

It might as well have been a funeral march down the stairs, we were all so sad and silent.

I held up the bag of Elvis's stuff to Agent Daniels.

He passed it to another guy and said they had to x-ray it before it came into the White House. I nodded. Elvis was going to a totally different world.

"Be sure to feed him well. He likes snacks and chicken-fried steak."

"I think we can handle that." Agent Daniels said it in a way that made me worry Elvis would never see another chicken-fried steak again.

Ripley walked up to me and sat down. I reached out and petted his head. He was soft, but not as soft as Elvis. And I felt a little guilty petting him right in front of Elvis.

Elvis walked up to Ripley. I understood what he said, but to everyone else it was just some low growling. "Benjamin is extremely important to me, and if I hear that anything has happened to him, you better watch out, because I'll come back and you'll be sorry."

"Elvis. Be nice."

"I'm watching you."

Ripley lowered his head. I patted him again to reassure him and whispered, "He's just being like that because he's sad to leave me. Don't take it personally." Ripley thumped his tail like he understood me.

My mom, Ripley, and I watched them leave from the bay window seat. Elvis peed on a few of our trees, which I think was more for Ripley than for anyone else. Right before he jumped into the back of the black sedan that was parked in the driveway, he turned back and looked over at us in the window.

We waved. And the tears started flowing again. And then we watched as Elvis threw his head back and howled. I have never heard a sound like that before, and I probably never will again.

"Awwwhoooooooooo!"

Elvis jumped into the car, and he was gone.

# 16

I couldn't help it. Suddenly I jumped off the window seat and ran toward the door. I threw it open and ran across the front yard so I could watch the tail-lights of the Secret Service cars making their way down the street. Ripley barked. My mom yelled at me not to run into the street, but I couldn't even think. I was too busy waving good-bye to Elvis. I didn't know if he saw me, but I didn't care. After I couldn't see the car with Elvis in it anymore, I sat down on the curb and put my head in my hands. I was no longer crying, but I had this big, empty feeling in my chest.

Pretty soon Ripley nuzzled my neck. His tongue was much smaller than Elvis's, and he had less slobber.

I looked at Ripley. Closely. Honestly. I hadn't paid much attention to him because I was so wrapped up in Elvis's departure, but now that I had a chance to check him out, I found him pretty cute. And he was half the size of Elvis. Oh, who am I kidding? He was a quarter the size of Elvis, if that.

"Hey, Ripley. So you had a detour to the White House, huh? How was the president?"

Ripley wagged his tail and panted.

"It's okay, boy, don't be shy. If you can talk, I'd rather know now than later." I stared him down. Nothing. Oh well, I guess my relationship with Elvis was one of those once-in-a-lifetime type things.

I scratched him behind his ears. He was a very nice dog. He seemed very friendly. See, this was me trying to be positive. No offense to Ripley, but he just wasn't Elvis. I mean, you had to see Elvis to even believe him. Without proof, it was like no one would even believe that his head was three times bigger than my head, so . . .

I shot up off the curb like a cannon. Ripley immediately started barking. I hoped nothing was about to happen with my brain right now, because I really had no time to lose.

"Mooooooom! Mom! Mom! Mom! Mom! Mom!

Moooooooom!" My mom ran toward me at warp speed with her arms outstretched.

"My baaaaby!" And soon she had me all scooped up in her arms. "There, there, Benji, let it out. Of course you're sad. I'm so sorry, honey. You can cry it out."

It took me a while to pull my face out of her chest (my mother, very strong), but then I yelled, "Put me down! We've got to go! Hurry!"

"Go where?"

"I don't have a picture of me and Elvis. We never took a picture. I have to have a picture!"

"I don't understand. What do you want to do?"

"I want you to chase the Secret Service down so we can get a picture. They can't be that far. They just left."

"Benji, I don't know if that's a good idea."

"Mom, we are going to go. Now. So get your keys. Please. This is important to me. He's changed my life. I need proof. Think about your scrapbook! Think about me!"

"Benji, baby, I know you're upset, but—"

"Mom, all my life you told me that you would do anything for me, and that you'd always be there for me when I needed you. You promised, and I believed you. Well, today's the day. I don't know how to explain it to you, but I need this. Please?"

"I'll get my keys." She sprinted across the front yard to get her purse. I ran to the car, beckoning Ripley to follow me. My heart was beating so loudly that at first I thought I was imagining the ringing in my ears, but I wasn't. I turned around and saw Alexander Chang-Cohen on his bicycle on the sidewalk behind me.

"Hey, Benji. Want to do homework together?" he asked.

"Alexander? Where did you come from?"

"Do you mean where are babies born? Or where do I live?"

"The second one."

"Oh, it turns out I live around the corner from you. I don't even have to cross the street, which is good, because I'm not technically allowed to cross the street unless it has a signal and a crosswalk."

"Alexander, you told me that already. Remember?"

"Right. But I thought we were pretending that never happened. At least that's what Taisy told me to do."

"Okay, fine, whatever. Look, I've got no time to talk. We have to chase down the Secret Service agents. Want to come?"

"Dude, I've waited my whole life to get such an invitation. Sure I want to come. But first I have to tell you something, and after I do, you might not want me to come anymore. But if you still do, your mom might have to call my mom from the car."

"Alexander, we don't have time for this. You can tell me on the way."

By this time my mom was running out the door with her camera and tripod (of course she'd bring her tripod. I could picture it now, a big portrait of us on the side of the highway). She unlocked the car door. Alexander dropped his bike in our front yard and looked straight at me.

"Benji, I'm not going anywhere until I say what I need to say. I can't take it anymore. I've been trying to tell you this all day. I'm the one who took your lug nut. It was me. I didn't steal it, though. I found it in the hallway when I was picking up all my stuff Billy threw everywhere. I don't know why I thought it was Billy's, but I did. So instead of returning it to him or putting it in the school's lost-and-found box like a responsible citizen, I put it in my pocket. And then, weirdly enough, I forgot about it until you brought it up. And when I heard it was your most prized possession, I panicked because I had no idea where it was anymore. For all I knew my mom washed my pants and threw it out in the trash. So all day I've been worried it would be all my fault if it's gone forever. Then when you and

Taisy blamed it on Billy, I went along with it because I thought that would buy me a little time to look for it. I never thought Taisy would go all Navy SEAL on us and insist we go over and storm the gates at Billy's house.

"I know I shouldn't have gone along with you thinking it was Billy who was responsible for losing it instead of me. But I liked you so much during lunch that I just couldn't bear being the guy who lost your good luck charm.

"When I finally got home, I found it in the laundry room. It may have shrunk a bit—the leather string, not the lug nut, obviously, since titanium doesn't shrink—but at least now it's extra shiny and cleaner than it was when I found it, and here it is.

Alexander held out his hand and opened it, revealing the missing lug nut at last. It sparkled in the sun, and just seeing it made me feel hopeful that we'd be able to catch up to Elvis and the Secret Service, even though Alexander's confession had just cost us another two minutes. Man, oh man, who knew so many words could even fit in such a tiny kid?

Alexander was still babbling on, "I'm so sorry I didn't tell you sooner, please don't hate me, but if you do, I understand, but it'll also make me really, really sad."

My mom spoke first. "Benji, is everything okay?"

I just smiled and nodded. "Mom, meet Alexander Chang-Cohen, Alexander Chang-Cohen, this is my mom. Alexander is new at school, he's my new best friend, and he's also a hero, since he found my lug nut for me!"

Her eyes welled up. I think if we weren't in such a rush, my mom would have cried herself. It was the first time I had ever brought a friend home from school.

We all buckled up, and Alexander asked if my mom could call his mom, because he really only had permission to be around the corner at our house. My mom called Alexander's mom on her car speakerphone. Alexander's mom sounded really happy that I was actually a real person, which meant Alexander probably didn't have many friends either. My mom, rather than getting into the long, crazy story of it all, decided to play it safe and told Alexander's mom that she was taking us for ice cream. She also invited Alexander over for dinner. Alexander's mom hesitated, but my mom said she would bring Alexander and his bicycle home, and she would love to meet her. She promised to bring some dessert.

I piped up and said my mom was the best baker in the entire neighborhood. Realtors even used her as a selling tool to get people to buy homes near us, because my mom is president of the Welcome Wagon.

Mrs. Chang-Cohen laughed and said her Realtor had told her about my mom and said those exact words, but she hadn't believed it at the time. My mom assured her that after one bite of her red velvet cake, she'd believe it.

"Mom, remember that time two years ago on April tenth when you were in the kitchen wearing your red sweater?" Alexander suddenly spoke up. "And I asked if I would one day have a friend who would invite me over to dinner at their house like I saw on television, and you said absolutely it would happen but you weren't sure when, and I said I didn't think it would ever happen, and you promised me it would, and then I asked why, and you said that when you make a best friend, you know it immediately? Well, when I met Benji today, I knew we'd be friends forever. So don't you think you have to say yes and make good on your promise? Please?"

There was a silence from the other end of the phone. My mom looked at me quizzically, and I mouthed, "Long story, tell you later." She nodded, and we all held our breath for Mrs. Chang-Cohen's response. I think it took so long for her to reply because she might have been crying, which meant our moms were definitely going to be fast friends.

"Sure thing, baby. And Mrs. Barnsworth, I look forward to meeting you later. And Alexander needs to eat all his vegetables, no complaints."

"Yes, Mom."

"Hi, Mrs. Chang-Cohen, I'm Benji," I said. "I just want you to know that I promise to eat all my vegetables too."

Mrs. Chang-Cohen laughed and said she looked forward to meeting Alexander's new best friend. After we hung up the phone, Alexander asked what was really going on, and I told him that we really were chasing down the Secret Service guys. I gave him the abbreviated version of the whole Elvis story (minus the talking dog part). After I finished talking, I looked at his face to see if he believed me, and he couldn't have looked happier.

"That's the best story ever. Now, Mrs. Barnsworth, which way are you going to the highway? Because I know all three routes, and I'm pretty sure that the Secret Service guys would take the second route, because it's more direct and . . ."

I explained to my mom that Alexander had total recall. "See, Alexander has a weird brain, just like me."

"You do not have a weird brain. And neither does Alexander. You're both just extra special. That's all.

Now Alexander, which way should I go?"

"I'd take Maple to Dogwood Lane, and then hit Route 309, which will lead to I-276, which is the most direct route to Washington, DC."

"That's amazing," I said in awe.

"I'm good with maps. I can see them in my head."

I looked out the window and saw that we were still waiting at the stoplight on Grand Street. My mom calls it the forever red light, because it seems like it lasts forever. I sighed. The more I thought about it, the more I wondered whether we'd ever catch up with them. We were at least ten minutes behind them. What if we never found them?

"Don't worry, Benji, we'll drive all the way to the White House if we have to." My mom looked at me in the rearview mirror. She always knew what was going through my head. Then I noticed a huge black Escalade at the Shell station up ahead.

"Mom, pull into the gas station."

"What? Why? We have plenty of gas."

"Just do it. Stop the car!" She slammed on the brakes, and Ripley flew into the back of the front seat, just like Elvis did the first time he drove with my mom.

I jumped out and ran over to the black Escalade. I couldn't believe our luck! It was Taisy's dad's car.

"Mr. McDonald! Hey! It's me, Benji!"

Taisy got out of the car.

"What's going on?"

"The Secret Service took Elvis to go live at the White House, and we're never going to see him again. After they left, I realized I didn't have a picture of him, so now we're going to get one. Do you want to come with us? This is your chance to say good-bye. I'm sure Elvis would like to say good-bye to you and Princess Daisy in person."

"Are you serious?" She looked closely at my face, and I was totally and completely serious.

"I don't have time to explain more. Do you want to come, or not?"

"Sorry, Benji, but Taisy has to get home and do her homework." Mr. McDonald got out of the car.

"Dad, we have to go! This is more important than homework. I'm going, and you're not going to stop me."

"Sorry, honey, but no can do."

"Daddy, I lied about my elbow hurting. I'm sorry, but I felt like I had no choice. You never listen to me. I've been telling you for the last two years that I didn't want to practice as much, that I wanted to do regular kid things and have fun. And today that's what I did, and it felt right. So listen, remember what you taught me about never letting down your team?"

"Sure I do."

"Well, this is my team, and I can't let them down when they need me the most." Taisy wasn't taking no for an answer.

"Mr. McDonald, this is kind of an emergency. I may never have this opportunity again," I said.

My mom got out of the car. "C'mon, we need to go now. Every minute we delay it'll be harder to catch up with them. By now they have fifteen minutes on us."

Taisy's dad looked at all our faces, and it was clear he was not happy about Taisy's big revelation. I've got to hand it to her, she really goes for broke sometimes. "Taisy, you lie to me again, and you're grounded for a month."

"Yes, Daddy."

Mr. McDonald then broke out into a big smile. "But I do respect you for standing up to me. I'm proud of you. And we'll figure it out later, together, okay? Now as for you parroting back what I always say to you about being a champion? Well, I'm glad you pay attention, because it's absolutely true: you don't become a champion by letting down your team. So let's go. I'll drive!"

"Mom?"

"At this point, who am I to say no to anything? Let's go."

In less than a minute, my mom parked her car at the gas station. We all piled into the Escalade. My mom sat in the front. Me, Taisy, and Alexander sat in the back, and Ripley was in the way back.

Once again, I told everyone the whole crazy story so Taisy and her dad were up-to-date. By this time we got on the highway, Taisy's dad was speeding. My mom recognized Taisy's dad and told him all about the twins' football career. She told him she was a big fan and remembered his famous catch, the one that won his team the Super Bowl the first time.

Taisy was very quiet. She was upset about Elvis leaving, and worried Princess Daisy wouldn't understand it. I said that Princess Daisy wasn't the only one, but that I knew it was fate for us all to be together like this when we went to find Elvis and say good-bye. What was truly amazing was having my pack. Me, Taisy, and Alexander weren't friends a week ago, but today, right now, it felt like we had been friends forever.

# 17

**Ripley barked like crazy** when he heard the sirens behind us. Alexander turned around and saw a police car with flashing lights behind us.

"Uh, Mr. Taisy's dad, I think you should pull over," said Alexander. I couldn't believe it. This was a disaster. We would never catch up to Elvis now.

"Don't worry. I have a special kind of relationship with cops. Meaning they treat me special and I'm always kind back."

After Taisy's dad posed for a picture with Officer Perkins and told him all about Elvis, we got back on the highway, only this time with a police escort. According to my calculations, with the new speed we were driving, we were only three minutes behind. That is, if Alexander was right about the route that they were taking, and if they didn't stop for gas or food. Taisy sensed my increasing anxiety. So did Ripley. He whined in the backseat.

"Benji, are you okay?" Taisy leaned into me.

"I don't think so. I'm really scared. What if we never find them? What if I don't ever see him again?"

"You know what that's called?"

"The ugly truth?"

"No, that's called stinkin' thinkin', and there's no place for that here," said Taisy. "I'm going to tell you what all my coaches tell me when I get stressed out because the clock is running out. And it's what I always think of when I start to feel negative. Are you ready?"

"Um, okay, tell me." Wow, Taisy sure could be dramatic.

"Just breathe and believe."

"That's it? That's what they say?"

"Breathe and believe. I know it sounds simple, but it works. You have to believe you can do anything, and that everything will work out how it's supposed to. Just believe. Breathe and believe. Breathe and believe."

I took a deep breath and thought about the last few days of my life, which were absolutely the craziest, most bizarre days I'd ever experienced. And today was the absolutely most incredible and most bizarre one of all. The highs, the lows, the drama, lots of laughs and lots of tears. It pretty much had everything.

"I believe." I said it quietly. Then I said it again, because I felt it. "I believe."

"I believe too," said Alexander.

"Me too. I always believe," said Taisy.

"I believe!" my mom called out from the front seat.

And then we all looked at Taisy's dad, whose giant hands gripped the steering wheel. "I believe . . . I believe . . . that I see them! Look, two black sedans up ahead!"

He was right. It was them. It had to be. He honked the horn at Officer Perkins, who saw the cars too. He put on his siren, and in no time at all we had caught up with them. The Secret Service cars pulled over to the side of the highway, Officer Perkins pulled his car behind them, and we pulled over behind the police car.

No one said anything, and no one knew what to do. After a moment, my mom kicked into action and opened her car door. She stepped out and marched toward the Secret Service cars.

"Should we get out too?" we asked.

Taisy's dad said we should wait. He said there was too much tension and far too many guns around for us to make any sudden movements. My mom had her head in the window of the second sedan for a while. She was talking nonstop, making wild hand gestures. After another thirty seconds, which felt like thirty years, she pulled her head out of the car and walked back. She stopped and talked to Officer Perkins, and then pulled him in for a big hug.

"Wait! Why are they leaving?" Alexander pointed up ahead. The two Secret Service cars were pulling away. When my mom opened the car door, everyone started talking at once. She held up her hand, and we all fell silent immediately.

"Everyone calm down. There's a rest stop two miles up, and we're all going to meet there. We can't have children and dogs on the side of a highway. It's too dangerous."

"Did you see him? Did you see Elvis? Was he okay?"

"Yes, I saw him, Benji. He was fine, as big as ever."

We followed Officer Perkins's car as it turned off the highway. My mom said he was coming with us because there was no way he was going to miss the excitement.

I was so happy at the thought of seeing Elvis again, I was speechless. Taisy was right. Everything had worked out. Well, not totally, since this was still going to be a good-bye, but at least I'd get a few pictures of

Elvis, which was all I really wanted.

It was a big reunion at the rest stop. If anyone had been watching, I'm sure they would never have guessed what the heck was going on. A police officer, four Secret Service agents, a retired Super Bowl football champion, my mom, Taisy, Alexander Chang-Cohen, and me, plus a giant dog, a medium-sized dog, and a tiny dog.

It was hard to tell whether Elvis was happier to see me or Princess Daisy. Then Elvis read my mind and said that he was really happy to see Princess Daisy, but he was even happier to see me. He was pretty choked up over the fact that I'd chased him down to say good-bye again. I told him that I knew I couldn't live my life without having a few pictures to remember him by. I said I planned to blow up the pictures to poster size and put them in my room. We took a few group shots of everyone, and yes, my mom had been very smart to bring her tripod. And yes, she did have problems with the remote. Luckily, Alexander is an electronics whiz, so he was able to help her with that.

My mom took some pictures of me, Taisy, and Alexander with all three dogs. And finally, at the end, she took a bunch of pictures of just Elvis and me. Elvis was so excited, I had to keep wiping the drool strands from his mouth. My favorite picture was when Elvis told me to climb on his back, and I hugged his neck and we both just smiled. Oh, there was also a good one of Taisy, Alexander, me, and Elvis where I made bunny ears behind him, but I'm pretty sure he wouldn't be thrilled with that one.

Even the Secret Service agents loosened up. Sure, Agent Daniels was a little cranky about getting further behind schedule, but he was really excited to meet Taisy's dad. It turned out Agent Daniels was a huge football fan. Taisy's dad let all the agents try on his Super Bowl ring, and of course in the back of his car he had a few footballs lying around that he signed for everyone to take home. It was probably the best hour of my entire life. Mainly because we had all been strangers just a day ago, and now we were all coming together in a big, crazy lovefest at a rest stop on the side of the highway.

I didn't cry when I said good-bye to Elvis this time. My mom had told Agent Daniels that we were definitely coming to Washington, DC, for a visit, with Alexander and Taisy, too. Taisy cried a little, but she said it was more because she knew how much Princess Daisy was going to miss Elvis.

It was getting dark, and my mom said it was time to go. Everyone got back in their cars, and it was just

Elvis and me alone in the rest stop park.

"I guess this is good-bye again?" I said.

"This is good-bye for just a little while. Until next time."

"I'll send you some of the pictures. Maybe they'll frame one and put it by your dog bed in the White House?"

"That would be great. But Benji, I don't need a picture to remember you. I'll remember you and our time together forever."

"Me too. Hey, you called me Benji."

"Yes, I guess I did."

"I love you, Elvis. And I want you to know that you're even more extraordinary than you think you are."

"I love you too, Benji, and don't kid yourself, you're pretty extraordinary too. You've got real character. And you found yourself a great pack."

"Yeah, I think so too. But there's always room for one more, so if the White House is too small for you, you always have a home with me."

I gave him one last big hug. He licked my face one more time, and then we parted ways. This time when we both got back to our cars, we turned at the same time and waved. It was just like the movies.

When I climbed back into the car, everyone was silent.

"I'm okay, guys. Really. I'm just happy we all got to be together again. And that I now have the pictures to prove it."

We drove home in silence. Everyone was lost in thought, but then when we got back to town, we all went out for hamburgers and ice cream.

When we switched back to our car, Taisy said she'd see me at school tomorrow during lunch.

"What do you mean?"

"I mean I'll save you a seat at lunch. Don't you want to sit together? You too, Alexander." I was so thrilled with the idea to have friends to sit with at lunch, I couldn't even say anything and just nodded. Alexander must have felt the same way, because we just stood there grinning like idiots and waving until she was gone.

Next we picked up Alexander's bike, and we brought Alexander and a cake to their house. My mom and Mrs. Chang-Cohen hit it off instantly, and my mom invited Mrs. Chang-Cohen to join her book club. Alexander said it was probably better not to tell his mom about our high-speed chase, and I agreed.

"You want to walk to school together tomorrow?" he asked when we said good-bye.

"Sure. Sounds good." We fist-bumped.

When we were in the car alone, I asked my mom what she was thinking, because she was so quiet. She said she was proud of me.

"Really? Why?" I asked.

"Just because, Benji. Just because."

# Acknowledgments

Writing alone is hard, but I was lucky enough not to be on my own for this labor of love. My dear friend Tasha Blaine, from that very first voicemail message you left telling me how much you loved Benji and Elvis, and how they made you laugh out loud on the subway—you became my number-one reader, supporter, and partner in this endeavor. You were the first eyes on every word, and I couldn't have done it without you. Lots of love and thanks to my family and friends, who have always supported my writing career: Mom; my big brother, John; my sister-in-law, Susie; the one and only Howard J. Morris; my most excellent friends Laura, Stephanie, Zander, Jessi, Holdy, Mark, and Jenna. Nadine Morrow and her amazing family must also be recognized. Nadine, you were absolutely the inspiration for the mom in this book! A very special shout-out must go to Sebastian Hochman and his dad, David. SB, you were my very first kid reader, and I thank you for your time and thoughts. Big thanks to my other early young readers: Ethan Plunkett and Sky Martin. I would also like to thank all my friends at *Shake It Up!*: the hilarious writing staff, the entire crew, everyone at the Disney Channel, and especially the world's best cast, because all of you helped me realize how much fun it is to write for children. Many thanks also to my awesome agent, Sally Wofford-Girand, to Mark Gordon and Josie Freedman at ICM, and my manager Alex Hertzberg. Last but never least, my fabulous, incredible editor, Alessandra Balzer; her wonderful associate editor, Sara Sargent; and the rest of her amazing team at Balzer + Bray and HarperCollins, who have been awesome partners in this whole exciting process. And to the talented Kelly Light, who brought the characters in this book to life perfectly. A big kiss to my furry dog family as well: Doozy, Finn, Kimba, and Wendell . . . I can't tell you how many times I've wished all of you could talk! And to all you Underdogs out there, remember: A good sense of humor is the key to life. Breathe and believe!

Read on for a sneak peek at the sequel,

# ELVIS
## AND THE
# UNDERDOGS
#### SECRETS, SECRET SERVICE, AND ROOM SERVICE

This story starts with me superglued to a window-seat cushion on a sunny Saturday in March. I know that sounds pretty crazy, but the way things work in my life, it's not that weird. Allow me to introduce myself: I'm Benjamin Wendell Barnsworth, but no one calls me that unless I'm in trouble. Most people just call me Benji. I'm the smallest kid in my fourth-grade class, but it doesn't bother me. Have you ever heard the expression "small kid, big personality"? No? Well, that's not surprising, because I just made it up. Sounds good, though, right? Now back to our regularly scheduled story.

One of my favorite places in our whole house is the window seat. I love it. It's right underneath a huge bay window that overlooks our front yard. In the afternoon, the sun pours in and makes me warm and cozy. I just lean my head back and pretty soon it's snooze city. This time, when I woke up from my nap, I couldn't move my legs. It totally freaked me out until I realized it wasn't actually my legs I couldn't move, it was my pants. But even that was a problem, since my legs happened to be in those very pants.

Upon further investigation, I discovered I couldn't move my pants because they were superglued to the window-seat cushion! It didn't take a genius to figure out my twin brothers, Brick and Brett, were to blame. How did I know it was them? Let's just say this wasn't the first time I woke up and found myself superglued to the window seat.

"Breeeetttt! Brickkkk! Get down here now!" I screamed.

"We're busy!! Why don't you come up here???" they yelled back, cracking themselves up.

"Ha! Ha! Very funny. You got me! Good one! You two better come down and help me remove my butt from this thing before Mom comes home, or all three of our butts are gonna be in huge trouble."

Normally, I don't get in trouble when the twins pull a stunt like this. My mom is loud and crazy, but she's fair. This was different. Ruining the seat cushion would end badly for everyone involved. Long silly story short, the twins had already ruined the other side of the cushion when they superglued me the first time and had to cut me out of my pants. We had used used the oldest trick in the book when you mess up a cushion. You flip it over! *Ta-done!*

So this time around it's not like we could just flip the cushion over. What were my brothers thinking? Did they think it was a magic three-sided cushion? Oh right, I keep forgetting. The twins never think!

Sometimes, as crazy as it sounds, I do wish I could be more like my brothers, because I have the opposite problem. I always think too much. In fact, sitting on the window seat is my favorite thinking place. And lately I've been sitting there a lot, because I really miss my dog Elvis. I know this might sound weird—that I can't forget this giant black Newfoundland dog who I only had for three days, and who technically wasn't even mine to begin with—but I can't help it. Those three days with Elvis changed my life forever. So I sit here and think about him and look out the window, past our front yard, all the way down the street. If I squint my eyes real hard, sometimes I can almost picture a tiny black speck way, way in the distance, and I imagine what it would be like if the speck got bigger and bigger and suddenly there was Elvis running up the street back home to me.

So there I was, literally stuck in my thinking-and-missing-Elvis spot, when my mom came home from the grocery store.

"Hey, Benji, baby, come help me with the groceries," she called out.

Uh-oh, how was I going to help her when I couldn't stand up?

"Sure thing, Mom. But uh, you see, funny story . . ." Oh boy, big brain of mine, don't fail me now. "I would, but I super miss Elvis and I'm so sad . . . it's like I'm paralyzed, and I can't move."

I wasn't exactly lying to my mom. I just wasn't telling her the whole truth. And it was by far the smartest thing I could have come up with. Here's the thing about my mom: She loves to share feelings. Her feelings, my feelings, my dad's feelings, the across-the-street neighbor's feelings, even total strangers' feelings. If you have feelings you'd like to share, my mother is the best listener ever. She says keeping your feelings bottled up, especially the sad or bad ones, gives you wrinkles. And since I don't want to be a wrinkly ten-year-old, and

4

when I share I usually get a snack, I'm pretty happy to open up to my mom on a regular basis.

My mom put a bag of groceries on the floor and bellowed for my brothers to unload the car. Then she pulled an ottoman over and sat next to me. The twins came down the stairs like they were running for a touchdown on the football field. They aren't the brightest, but even they knew my mom coming home wasn't a good thing. Without saying a word, they barreled out the front door to get the groceries. Or maybe they were running away, leaving me to deal with this sticky situation. (Sticky, get it?)

"Tell me everything. What's wrong, Benji?" my mom asked, putting her hand on my knee.

"I really, really miss Elvis, and sometimes I sit here and hope he's going to come back to me. I know that's never gonna happen, but I can't help it. And I thought it'd get better because it's been so long, but lately it seems worse."

I took a deep breath. Sure, I was praying my mother wouldn't realize I was superglued to the cushion, but what I said was actually 100 percent true, and it felt good to get it off my chest. My mom didn't seem the least bit surprised by what I said. I could tell because I'm pretty good at reading the furrows in her forehead.

Different ones pop up depending on whether she's worried, mad, hungry-cranky, or regular-cranky.

"Benj, honey, it's totally and completely normal for you to miss Elvis. He was a very special dog. And even though you only had him for a few days, he was your first dog. And everyone always remembers the firsts the most. Like I remember your first step, your first word, your first haircut, and your first loose tooth."

"The first time I ended up in the hospital emergency room?"

"Well, that's one of the firsts I actually try to forget. But all the good firsts in your life are really important, and you'll remember them your entire life."

My mom was not kidding about remembering all my firsts, because she's what you would call a power scrapbooker, meaning you better watch out when she's doing it, because she's got a hot glue gun and she's not afraid to use it—on everything.

"Hey, where were you when you had your first banana split? Do you remember?" she asked.

"With you," I answered immediately. Did I remember? Did I remember? Of course I remembered. I remembered like it was yesterday. We were down the Jersey Shore on vacation, and I was about four years old. My brothers were out on the beach doing the normal fun stuff you do when you're on vacation, while I was covered from head to toe in pink medicated lotion because I had an allergic reaction to the hotel sheets and I had a horrible red rash pretty much everywhere.

Since I couldn't be out in the sun, my mom and I were stuck in our beachside motel room together watching television, and then the television just died on us. Like there was this crackling sound, it went briefly to static, and then it just went black. My mom started laughing and said, "When it rains, it pours, doesn't it, Benji, baby?"

I didn't know what she was talking about, because it wasn't raining. In fact, it was a perfectly sunny day out. Then she said it was time for the two of us to make our own vacation fun. She put one of my dad's huge flowery Hawaiian shirts on me, and she rubbed pink lotion all over her own arms and face so I wouldn't feel like I was the only one who looked funny.

Together we finally left that boring hotel room and walked straight to the ice cream shop on the board-walk. It had this cool green mermaid statue holding up an ice cream like she was the fishy underwater version of the Statue of Liberty. Everyone stared at us like we were crazy. Well, they looked more at my mom, but everyone always looks at her because she has really big blond curly hair.

"Two banana splits, please!" she said when it was time to order.

The waiter immediately explained that their banana splits were really big, so it'd be better if we shared one. And without missing a beat, she told him we were aliens from the planet Calamine, researching desserts on Earth, and our planet had a strict policy against sharing when it came to desserts. In fact, they had a policy against moderation in general.

That banana split was the most beautiful thing I had ever seen. The vanilla scoop was on the left, followed by the chocolate scoop, then the strawberry scoop on the end. There was hot fudge, caramel, and strawberry sauce, at least two inches of whipped cream, and chocolate sprinkles. It was my first banana split. And yes, I will remember it forever.

"Oh, I get it now," I said, licking my lips at the memory. "So you're saying since Elvis was my first dog, he's extra special, and that's why I miss him so much?"

"Exactly. And that's okay. And that's why you still feel sad."

My mom was right. I only had Elvis for three days, but he was my very first dog. Now I had Ripley. He's the dog I was supposed to get in the first place, but due to a mix-up, I got Elvis instead. Ripley is a yellow Lab, and he's the complete opposite of Elvis, meaning that he's only sixty pounds instead of two hundred, he's white instead of black, and his fur is short and coarse instead of long and silky with a white star emblazoned right on his chest. Elvis has this lion mane around his chest, but I never told him that, because it would have gone to his head, like he was King of the Jungle. Trust me, Elvis already has a big enough opinion of himself.

Ripley is really sweet, and he always listens to me. Sometimes I think he can tell what I'm thinking before I even say it. Like how I sometimes forget to turn my bedroom light off, and right as I'm about to get up out of the bed to do it, Ripley just bounds across my room and jumps up on the wall and flips the light switch off for me. Elvis never listened to me, always had an opinion about everything, constantly ordered me around, and he once threw me out of a window at school. But the biggest difference between Ripley and Elvis is that Elvis can talk.

Yes, talk.

I know, I know, everyone has that reaction at first. Dogs don't talk in real life. Dogs only talk in comic strips, cartoons, television, and movies. I get that, you get that, but the way I see it, no one ever told that to Elvis—not that it would have mattered anyway, because I doubt he would have listened. Because he did talk, at least to me. I'm the only boy I've ever heard of who can talk to a dog. It might be because I had a seizure at school and passed out, which is why I needed to get a specially trained therapy dog like Elvis in the first place and why I got Ripley after him. A therapy dog can help me if I ever have a seizure again or another medical crisis. I figure maybe when I fell down and hit my head on the very hard hallway floor of my school, it caused my brain to be able to understand this one particular dog.

"Benji, earth to Benji, come in. Are you feeling better now?" My mom shook my leg, and for a second I got worried she'd realize it was superglued.

I nodded my head yes and gave her a smile. It was true. I did suddenly feel better talking about Elvis. "I do. Thanks, Mom. Hey, can I ask you one more thing?"

"Anything."

"Do you think it hurts Ripley's feelings that I still write letters to Elvis and that I miss him so much?" At the mention of his name, Ripley, who was lying below me on the floor, lifted his head. My mom petted him and shook her head.

"I think Ripley understands and is totally fine with it. He knows it doesn't mean you love him any less. Now, show me some love, okay?" And with that she leaned forward and gave me one of her big mama bear hugs. It was such a great hug that I temporarily forgot about my other situation, but I remembered it soon enough, because as she hugged me, she stood up. And when she stood up, she lifted me up along with the window-seat cushion. Uh-oh!

Right then the twins walked back in the door with the last of the groceries. They took one look at me getting hugged with the cushion stuck to my butt, dropped the bags on the floor, and ran back out the door.

"Whaaaaaaaat diiiiiidddddd you twooooooo doooooooo?!!!" my mom yelled, and since I was still in her arms, it was really, really loud.

My mom ripped me off the cushion, and I took some of the fabric with me on my pants. Then she had the same thought we did the first time this happened. She flipped the window-seat cushion over, which was when she saw the other messed-up side. And then there was even more yelling.

As punishment, she made the twins skip their pickup basketball game with their friends, which really bummed them out, because they live and breathe sports. They might not think, but they do know how to move, and they pretty much do it constantly.

But that wasn't the only punishment my mother gave out. It got worse. Much, much worse. She also said we now had to do one of our least favorite things in the world, which is to go to Macy's and watch her shop for a new seat cushion. All three of us begged and pleaded, but to no avail.

"If one of you complains for even a second more, I'll make you pay for this cushion!" she said.

That shut us up immediately. Twenty minutes later I had on a new pair of pants, and I climbed into our SUV with Ripley and my brothers, and we silently headed to the mall. As my mom drove, I looked out the window, and even though I was petting Ripley, I found myself thinking of Elvis again.

Here's another thing you should know about Elvis. He prefers to be called by his full name: Parker Elvis Pembroke IV, and it's probably what they call him where he lives now. But I never called him that, mainly because I knew it bugged him, but also because, to me he really seemed more like an Elvis.

I didn't even realize this until the Secret Service showed up at my house to take him back, but Elvis's initials spell out the word "pep." That just makes me laugh, because Elvis is the least peppy dog I know. If I had to describe Elvis in one word, I think grumpy-know-it-all-cranky-pants would probably be it.

You're probably wondering why I just threw the words "Secret Service" in there. Here's what happened. Elvis ended up at my house by accident. After he was born and trained at a farm in Tennessee, he was supposed to go live in the White House as the dog of the president of the United States! But instead there was a mix-up, and a giant crate of Elvis was delivered to my house on Fernbrook Lane in Pennsylvania. Eventually, they all figured out the mix-up, and after a few days the Secret Service showed up with Ripley, who was supposed to be my original therapy dog. What could I do? The president wanted his dog. I had to give Elvis back.

I write letters to Elvis at the White House, but I don't tell anyone except my mom, and that's only because I don't have a choice. She supplies the stamps. She also tracked down Agent Daniels, the lead Secret Service guy who picked up Elvis from our house. He thought she was joking when she asked him to read my letters, but once you hear my mom's does-it-sound-like-I'm-joking? voice, you can tell immediately she's not. So he tried to blackmail her for her award-winning red velvet volcano cake recipe, which is the cake she served him when he came for Elvis. Lucky for us, Agent Daniels was thinking about my mom's cake as much as I was thinking about Elvis.

My mom refused to give up her recipe (she got it from her mother, who made her promise to pass it down to only one person in her life), but she promised she'd FedEx Agent Daniels one cake every month if he read Elvis my letters.

Agent Daniels emailed my mom to say he's become quite the popular guy at work because he shares at least half of her cake with the other Secret Service agents. He said every time the cake arrives at the White House, Elvis drops whatever he's doing and takes off running. I like to think it's not because he smells the cake, but because he's waiting for the letters from me that come with it. But it's probably not true. If me and a cake were drowning in a lake at the same time, I'm not sure if Elvis would know which to save first. I can even hear his voice: "Benjamin, I have at least a few minutes to save you. A cake goes soggy very quickly indeed."

The funny thing is that Elvis can't even have any of the cake because there's chocolate in it, but my mom always throws in one cupcake that's the same recipe but without the chocolate just for him. So now I've written Elvis one letter a week for the three months, two weeks, and two days that he's been gone.

"Hey, Mom, did you get stamps today? But if you didn't, that's fine too," I called out from the back of the SUV.

I hadn't mailed my latest letter yet because I was waiting for my mom to get some new cool stamps. I always like the special-edition stamps that the post office puts out. If you're going to have your letter inspected carefully because it's going to the White House, you might as well make sure it has a good-looking stamp on it.

"I did." She sighed. I could tell she was still upset about the cushion.

"Did they have some cool ones?"

"They did." She looked straight ahead, not even glancing in her rearview mirror at me. She turned to my brother who was sitting next to her in the passenger seat. "Brick, go into my purse and don't touch anything except the little paper envelope that has the stamps in it. Pull them out and hand them to Benji."

"Yes, Mom." Brick reached into my mom's purse and handed me the stamps. "Hey, Mom, can I have some gum?"

"What do you say?"

"May I have some gum, please?" Brick asked again,

using his best good-boy voice.

"No, you may not," my mom replied, using her best don't-pretend-to-be-a-good-boy-when-you're-not-one voice.

Whoa, withholding a stick of gum meant she was really mad. I almost felt sorry for Brick. Almost.